THE SOUL TRADE

Judas Investigations: Book One

Edward Rose

*To everyone with a story just waiting to
be let loose upon the world...*

CHAPTER 1

"Oh shit, shit, shit...", I swore through gritted teeth. "This time I'm really going to die."

A fiery ball of plasma smashed into the wall only inches from my head at the very instant I stumbled and fell hard to the ground. Even then, the heat blast was enough to singe the tips of my hair and strip the skin off one side of my face. I would love to say some kind of sixth sense had warned me of my imminent death, but my skin-of-the-teeth escape was more due to catching my foot on a loose slab, slamming on the ground with all the grace of a drunken hippo.

The area of wall closest to me was now reduced to a molten orange sludge spilling rapidly across the floor, so it was a safe bet that whatever had just been hurled in my direction was even hotter than the one thousand or so blistering degrees required to produce the bricks in the first place.

My sudden and totally unplanned dive had left both knees and the palms of my hands skinned raw. Painful, but not desperate. A much bigger worry was the aching part of my anatomy that used to be my stomach, now alarmingly warm and oozing blood inside my shirt.

Another curse escaped my lips, silently this time. If I'd known the case I was asked to investigate involved a Wrath Daemon, I would have brought a more powerful weapon. There again, being completely honest, I'd have refused to take it on and you'd find me sitting in the comparative safety of my office, concentrating my efforts on drinking myself into a warm, fuzzy oblivion.

Momentarily distracted by a surge of self-pity and an overwhelming and inappropriately timed desire for a decent bourbon, I almost missed the huge cloven hoof suddenly looming over me, and only just rolled out of the way in the nick of time.

The flagstone I'd been sprawled over a second earlier shattered with an ear-splitting crack, a stray splinter of the dislodged stone managing to carve a deep cut into the small part of my face that had so far survived the day relatively unscathed.

Don't get me wrong, I'm not naturally vain, but it'd be nice to sometimes end the day without looking like I'd stuck my head in a bag full of angry scorpions.

"Damn it..."

As the giant limb lifted for a second attempt at pulping my head, I wiped one hand across my face, smearing blood and grit. Without pausing, I brought my palms crashing together, hurting like hell, shouting a short, but incredibly potent, hex. The air just above my face shimmered brilliantly and the descent of the hoof was arrested suddenly and absolutely as it made contact with the radiating wall of power I had summoned.

Wincing at the sound of shattering bone as I scrambled awkwardly to my feet, I looked down at the grimacing, pained face of the Daemon that, until now, had been hunting me.

It had been expecting an easy kill. Instead, it found itself blasted with Magick, which in the City is rarer than rocking-horse shit. It's about the same odds as a cat cornering the only mouse in the City who, it turns out, has a serious steroid addiction and owns a chainsaw.

Clutching at its leg with one grotesque, sinewy hand, it glared furiously, while the other deformed hand flexed and twitched as another of the huge balls of plasma started forming between the long, gnarled fingers. Considering the recent shift in circumstances, you had to admire its commitment.

"You... mistake," it snarled, pulling its arm back and preparing to hurl the fireball straight at me. Big and tough they might be, but not all that literate. This one had managed part of a sentence, which probably made it a contender for Wrath Daemon Poet Laureate... lucky me.

Before the creature's arm completed its arc, I'd pulled my gun from its holster behind my back, snapping off two shots in quick succession. The first hit the Daemon's arm, completely severing the monster's hand, the glowing ball of fire fizzling away and leaving nothing but a smoking damp patch that smelled disgusting. The second shot ended the creature's misery, or at least sent it back to whatever nasty underworld realm it had come from, where its misery was likely to continue. Daemons don't forgive failure.

Neither are they all that keen on breathing, smiling, eating too many carbs after midday, and cats.

The thing about cats is actually true. I'll explain later if I remember.

Within moments there was almost no sign that an eight-foot-tall, otherworldly sociopath had ever been there. All that was left was a slightly discoloured stain spread across the stone floor... and quite a lot of my blood.

At that point, my legs decided to give up on me. Only the harsh comfort of the wall at my back kept me sitting anywhere even close to upright.

Deciding to use my time as efficiently as possible, I split my concentration between continuing to bleed slowly on to the floor and updating my notebook, the new mark in the 'kill' column nearly completing the page.

I was still slumped there nearly three hours later when the janitor found me, and he was not at all happy about the mess.

CHAPTER 2

When I staggered into the small flat behind the office, still bleeding more than I would have liked, Samson was there waiting for me. He had that special look on his face that only cats and angry exes can manage. It's a look that states very clearly that they're only there out of the goodness of their hearts, not because of anything you're bringing to the relationship, and that I would be reminded of this act of charity... repeatedly.

He nodded towards the leather recliner that served as chair, bed, and occasional surgery; then stalked off to the far side of the room as I managed a last few clumsy steps before collapsing heavily into the recliner's clammy embrace. The last thing I heard as I succumbed to the welcoming darkness was the sound of Samson padding his way back over to me, muttering to himself in annoyance.

Samson is a Norwegian Forest Cat, large, fluffy, and an absolute top-tier asshole. If you didn't know any better you might think he belongs to me, but we agreed early on in our relationship that we wouldn't use archaic terms like owner or pet, partly because he's obviously smarter than me, but mainly because he bit a chunk out of my hand the first time I tried.

I think the name Samson is a reference to his long hair. Certainly, the only time I took him to get his fur trimmed, he claimed he felt too weak to do anything other than eat and sleep for the next week, although I couldn't see how that was any different from his regular behaviour. If nothing else, it was another example of whoever is responsible for handing out the names here having a good laugh at our expense.

The one thing he and I agree on is that he probably wasn't a cat in his previous life, although after that our opinions diverge. Samson is convinced that he was someone rich and powerful. I think he must have been about the worst person who ever lived. To come back as anything other than a human is rare... really rare. Samson is one of just a handful of sentient creatures living in the City, which must make for a pretty lonely existence. It doesn't excuse his incredible levels of assholery, but it does help explain it. Bottom line is, we'll probably never know the truth. Just like everyone else in this place, Samson has no recollection of his previous life.

When I woke up it was to the sight of him biting through a loose thread, hanging from the end of a haphazardly stitched wound across my stomach.

I think he could sense my silent critique of his handiwork, stopping to give me an annoyed look.

"You do realise that I'm a cat, not a sodding surgeon, don't you?"

His expression of wounded pride was rather undermined by the fact he still had a length of thread hanging from his mouth, but he continued unperturbed.

"Frankly, the fact that I got you stitched up at all is pretty amazing." He raised a paw and waggled it in my direction. "You try doing this without thumbs."

"Sure, you're a genius."

"I even cleaned the wound first," he added, "which was no bed of roses. No offence but your blood tastes like shit."

Trying unsuccessfully to reassure myself that cat saliva was sterile, I ignored his last comment and levered myself into an upright position... which hurt.

"So, what did I miss while I was out?"

With a long-suffering sigh, Samson padded across to the

bureau, nudging open the small ledger balanced precariously among the other piles of random crap, scraps of paper, and discarded food boxes that made up my filing system.

"Let's see, there was a missing person... uhm... ah yes, and a confused young lady who claimed to be lost. Before you ask, I checked, and the cases were not related. The missing person is a six-foot-tall, five-foot-wide grunt who goes by the charming name of 'Boiler', whereas the young woman was a tiny little thing who apparently couldn't remember what her name was. But if I had to guess I would go with something classic like 'Hope'."

I'm pretty sure cats aren't supposed to blush, but there was some sort of blossoming pinkness beneath Samson's fur. Normally, the only things in life that Samson cared about were football, curry, and the occasional foray into exotic catnips. Whoever this mysterious woman was, she'd certainly made an impression.

In most circumstances, the opportunity to take the piss out of my furry flatmate would have been too tempting to pass up, but even though I heal fast, I was still missing a sizeable proportion of my red blood cells. The choice was either to stay up and needle Samson – with a reasonable chance I would either pass out or die – or do the sensible thing, get my head down, and give my broken body a chance to recover.

Three hours later, I finally fell into bed, pretty close to complete physical collapse but with the warm glow of a job well done, leaving Samson curled in a furious grump in his basket.

I was hoping for the blissful blankness of deep sleep, but karma wanted to teach me a lesson for being a dick, and instead of resting my brain as I'd hoped, my thoughts wouldn't stop bouncing all over the place, like a pinball in a machine being played by a really angry octopus with fidgety fingers.

A weird analogy, as I'm pretty sure octopuses don't even have fingers, but I guess that's what having no proper sleep for three nights in a row, while fighting Daemons, does to your brain.

So, while I wait for the stuff in my head to calm down, and my body does its whole 'healing' thing, let me set you straight on a few points. It'll save time later.

My name is Judas, or that's what people have called me ever since I arrived in the City. It's not my real name, but I couldn't even begin to guess what that might be. I've been Judas for as long as I can remember.

Same as with Samson, I presume it's some kind of joke to someone out there. Whoever it is that pulls the levers in this place. After a while, I added Patrick, thinking it might take the edge off the whole Judas thing, plus it kind of felt right. Judas might be what this place chose for me, but Patrick was all my own.

When you arrive, pretty much the only thing you know is your name, and it always means something. Mine means I did something really bad. Something I need to pay for. I don't know what it was, but I do know it's left me stranded in the City for as long as I can remember. I've seen plenty of people arrive and leave over the years, but I seem to be stuck, constantly reliving the same mistakes, or – if I'm feeling particularly creative – coming up with brand new ones.

I remember Father Trent telling me the story of Sisyphus. It's not a biblical tale, but I guess he felt the parallel was just too good to pass up. He was cursed by the gods to push the same boulder up a mountain day after day, an impossible task that he was doomed to attempt, and to fail, until the end of time. I could kind of see what he meant. Although in my case the boulder was more like a giant ball of red-hot razor blades, and most days I was too drunk, tired, or generally pissed off to try. Aside from that, it was a perfect parallel.

Like I said, what I did must have been seriously bad. It's the only explanation for the recurring shit-show that is my life.

Either that, or I just keep making deliberately bad decisions, like a moth enthusiastically battering itself to death on a lightbulb.

I've had a few occasions, deep into the night when I couldn't sleep and the worst parts of my brain take over the wheel, when I wished I could remember what I'd done, but most of the time I'm grateful for the empty void.

The closest I've come is just after I wake up, in the panicky moments of horrible clarity we all exist in for a couple of seconds before our brains do their job and rationalise away all that randomised guilt and existential dread. A couple of times I've glimpsed jagged snippets of another life, but never enough for it to make any sense. It's like looking at a single piece of a jigsaw, but with no corner pieces, edges, or pictures on the box to refer to.

Everyone else here is the same, no-one knows who they were before. It's a strange state to exist in, and one that affects people in different ways.

Some try to live a good life, save up enough positive karma to get a ticket out and head on up to the pearly gates, or whatever else it is they believe is out there waiting for them. They normally try to keep their heads down, staying in close-knit communities that have turned their backs on the wilder excesses the City has to offer. It's very rare that one of these 'good' people ends up in a position of authority or prominence. This isn't the kind of place where virtue is rewarded.

Then there are the individuals who've settled in for the long haul. You can tell the 'lifers'. They tend to have a bleak sense of humour, a predisposition towards drink, and the ability to see the worst in everything. For most, this is a conscious decision, concluding that whatever troubles they face in the City are better than the uncertainties of leaving, but there are also a few exceptions like me. We're the ones who don't stay through choice. Instead, we're stuck here – whether we like it or not.

The third group are even worse. They're the cause of

three-quarters of my business and all of my more interesting scars. Rather than try and build up a stockpile of good behaviour, they get so sick of the daily grind that they embrace whatever darkness brought them here and let it consume them completely. It guarantees them an eventual way out of the City, but it's not a route I would recommend. I caught a glimpse of the 'other place' once, and there is no way in hell I'm ever going any where near there again.

That's where I come in. I'm officially the City's number one private investigator, the best there is. I'm also the worst... and the only, but I eventually decided to go with 'best' in my advertising.

When the entire population of a City is there because they behaved badly in life, you can bet there will be plenty of unsavoury secrets for an old-fashioned style gumshoe to dig into. Bad habits are exactly that, difficult to shake off, even after going through a life-changing experience... like dying.

This brings me to the biggest thing you should know about the City. As you can probably tell from the subtle hints I keep dropping, this place is occupied by people who have already lived... and died at least once. There's no hidden reveal here, this place is Purgatory, pure and simple. The middle floor in the great after-life elevator. When it's time to leave, you either go up or down, and it's a one-way trip.

I might have been here longer than most, but I arrived the same way as everyone else, waking up deep inside the bowels of a huge old hospital high on a hill, right on the outskirts of the City, even further out than Old Town. All I was wearing was a grubby hospital gown, with nothing to identify me, other than a wristband with my given name scribbled in blue biro, 'Judas'.

The hospital was a sprawling, gothic monstrosity of a place, completely abandoned for as long as anyone could remember. Now it functioned as a gloriously creepy arrivals lounge.

A few well-meaning individuals had tried for a while to spruce the place up. They had even set up a rota system, with volunteers sitting and waiting for newly arrived souls, with the admirable intention of welcoming them and helping them settle into their new life in the City. They hoped it would ease the trauma of waking up in the creepiest building this side of Norman Bates' dressing-up room. It didn't last for long.

Firstly, quite a few of the people who end up in the City are, by default, really horrible bastards. Secondly, finding yourself in a creepy old Gothic hospital shortly after your own death can be a pretty traumatic experience. I think it was about the third time a benevolent volunteer was almost forced to eat their own limbs by a newly awakened, panicking psychopath, that the whole volunteer system got well and truly shut down.

After that, people were left to deal with things on their own. Which is exactly how things were when I arrived. It's not a happy memory, and I don't like to think about it too much, but I would say I screamed for a couple of minutes, then realised that if someone did respond to the sound of screaming in an abandoned and exceedingly creepy hospital, they might not be the kind of person I wanted to meet. So, I stopped and put my energy into trying to find a way out.

It was dark by the time I found the main exit, with a constant torrent of rain adding to my misery. I didn't realise at the time that dark and rainy was pretty standard, sometimes with a bit of fog thrown in for added atmosphere, but it did mean that the lights of the City were the only thing you could make out for miles around, so that's where I headed.

A lot has happened since then, so I'll keep to a few highlights.

Jump forward five years and, although I was still a million miles away from the cynical old bastard that I am now, I was also no longer the wide-eyed innocent who stumbled into the City and across the threshold of Mrs Jones' club, searching for those most basic of human requirements – some food, warmth, an explanation of what the hell was going on and, if possible, something to wear other than a backless hospital gown.

I had just opened the office, with grand plans for the future. Back then, the 'Judas Investigations' sign emblazoned across the glass of the doorway was still fresh and new, separating my little kingdom from the rest of the run-down block I would be calling home.

There had been a desk for me, another for the reception, and a third for my future business partner. Or at least, once things took off and I needed someone to share my success with. I know it might all sound a bit naïve, but seriously, how hard should it be to run a private sleuthing agency in Purgatory? I'd seen enough in those first five years to know that the City had more than its share of dodgy dealers, grifters, cheats and scumbags to keep me busy.

To start with, things had gone pretty well. Oddly, no-one had thought to set up a detective agency until my arrival, and there was plenty of demand. Normal stuff mainly, checking out spouses who were up to no good, keeping tabs on employees who were suddenly living far better lives than their wages should support, or running surveillance for some of the more cut-throat corporates.

But a lot of dirty water has passed under the bridge since then. The other seats in the office were never filled, or at least not for long. The sign lost its sparkle, and the big money cases never materialised. I was the only constant, stuck in a city that wouldn't let me go, working case after case for the kind of people I would normally cross the road to avoid.

Which brings me right back around to how I ended up running into a Wrath Daemon. I had been hired to follow a newly married, recently blonde, possible gold-digger, now going by the unfortunate name of Mrs Creech. Her husband wanted me to find out whether she was staying true to her marriage vows, and so I had spent most of the evening sat outside her health club, recording anyone else who was arriving or leaving during her stay.

As far as I could tell, Mr Creech didn't genuinely suspect his new wife of anything, he was just a very thorough kind of guy, and so rich that paying out for a few days of my time didn't even register. It was easy, mindless, and theoretically completely safe work, so it had rather caught me by surprise when a huge, gnarled arm had smashed through the window of my car.

The damage to the car wasn't a big deal. It's so rusty and run down, it can't devalue any further. You could crush the whole thing down to an ugly paperweight and it would still be worth the same. But, as I was dragged through the window, I snagged an important part of my guts on the broken glass, which was a problem.

I try to avoid fighting with Daemons whenever possible. They're very big, extremely nasty, and tend to hold a grudge. Seeing as they're also extremely hard to kill, it's better not to piss them off, but if one is holding you in the air with one arm and trying to pull you in half with the other, you don't have much of a choice.

Still, I had decided to start off friendly, settling for pulling both my legs up and booting the creature in its ugly mug. With that many teeth, you would think I'd have managed to knock at least a couple loose, but it just made my new pal even angrier.

With a dismissive grunt, it had swung its arm and thrown me across the street, my flight interrupted by a pile of rubbish bags. Unfortunately, they were stored inside a large metal dumpster, so it hurt like hell, but at least the thing had let me go.

I'm not the greatest fighter in the world, but I've been stuck in this place long enough to learn a few tricks, one of which is how to get my ass kicked. I'm pretty good at it by now, so, rather than lying on the ground and whimpering pathetically, which I think is what the Daemon had been expecting, I was up on my feet and running towards the nearest doorway within moments. Don't get me wrong, there would still be whimpering, but I'd decided to save that for a better time.

Which is pretty much where we came in... fireball... gunshot... bleeding for a bit... a quick stagger back to the office... trying to sleep... and here we are.

CHAPTER 3

I should have learned by now, if something appears to be too good to be true, then it is. I'm pretty sure that used to be the case back when I was alive, and it's even more true now.

It was early in the morning, or at least I had just woken up, peeling my face off whatever it was that was living on the top of my desk. The first thing I saw was a small bottle of cheap whisky. It was still half full, which I felt pretty good about. The other two empty bottles... not so much.

After a few hours, I had given up on getting to sleep via the old-fashioned method, deciding that a quick drink would help me on my way. Seems like I had followed that with another couple of quick drinks, and then some not-so-quick ones.

There was a shape in front of me, wavering slightly as my eyes took a determined run-up to focusing properly. Slowly the outline resolved itself into a woman. She was young, maybe early twenties, dark hair tightly curled and framing a wide, friendly face that looked like it was made for smiles, but which hadn't had the chance to practice much recently.

"Mr Judas?"

Her voice was warm and mellifluous, the hint of a lisp only adding to the caramel smoothness of her speech.

I nodded... slowly. Anything more energetic seemed likely to dislodge the inside of my head or stomach.

"I was told that you help people... that you might be able to help me." The look on her face said different. She was obviously finding it hard to believe I was capable of helping myself, let alone anyone else.

Spurred on by wounded pride, I managed a non-committal grunt. I had been planning on maybe trying a word or two, but the nod had really taken it out of me.

Unperturbed, my visitor carried on talking, reading my silence as an encouragement to continue. I was happy to let her. There was something soothing about the way she spoke, not just her voice, but the fact that she genuinely seemed to believe I could help her, despite my current state and all evidence to date suggesting very much the contrary.

"Let me get straight to the point, Mr Judas. I turned up here just over two days ago. One minute I was at home in my flat, just about to feed my dog. Then there was a flash... and pain," she shuddered, the recollection obviously not an easy one, "and the next thing I knew I was here, waking up in some creepy hospital."

I had another go at speaking, managing to force out my first word of the day. Fortunately, it was a really good one.

"So?"

"Mr Judas, I don't know how I got here. I don't recognise this city, not a single street, not a single person. I can't remember anything before feeding my dog... and even that feels like a dream now. None of it makes any sense. I've tried talking to people and they just look at me like I'm crazy... but I'm not... I know I'm not... I..."

Her rush of words wound down, and with a sigh, she finally sat down in the chair opposite mine. I've seen it plenty of times, recent arrivals struggling to accept their new reality, although she seemed more perturbed than most. It's not the kind of case I take on, because there is no answer.

"I'm not..." she managed again, trying to sound firm, before leaning forward and resting her head in her hands. I thought for a minute she was going to cry, but she didn't, just

15

rubbed her forehead like she was trying to scrub away a persistent headache.

"So, my cat tells me you can't remember your name," I said, taking pity on my guest and deciding I would help share the strain of conversation. It wasn't a sentence I would normally open with, but I was pretty pleased with myself for having managed the whole thing without either being sick or passing out, so I marked it down as a win.

She lifted her head from her hands for a moment, the look of confusion on her face so comical that it very nearly made me smile.

"What?"

"You were here yesterday?" I said. "Or at least I presume it was you… You met my cat."

"That's right," she replied, "but I was just talking to myself, I didn't think that your cat was listening… or could understand me." She started rubbing her temples again, a slow circling motion that didn't seem to be doing much other than moving her hair around. "Horrible creatures, constant rain, talking cats… this place is so weird."

"And when you woke up in the hospital, you didn't have a name tag on your wrist?"

"No… why? Should I have?"

She still had the slightly dazed look of the newly landed, a sure sign that they were still fresh enough to be surprised, troubled or disgusted by their surroundings. Occasionally you would also see an arrival who seemed to be more delighted than anything else. They were the ones to watch, preferably from a safe distance. Either that, or just shoot them straight away. It was likely to save you time in the long run.

It might sound like I'm a bit blasé about the whole shooting people thing, but I'm not. The kill list at the back of my diary might be pretty full, but I've been here for a really long time.

When I first arrived, I was pretty squeamish about violence. Hell, during the first couple of weeks I was here, I don't think I killed anyone at all.

But this place gets under your skin, brings out your worst impulses, or at least it tries to, and it seems I have an uncontrollable impulse to shoot Daemons, monsters and assholes.

Which made my visitor all the more unusual. Over time I've developed a sixth sense for troublemakers. As the only private eye in the worst city north of Hell, I've had plenty of difficult customers come through that door.

I've seen more than my fair share of tall, blonde, soon-to-be widows and widowers, with transparent tales about their elderly, but frustratingly healthy partners. I've crossed swords (figuratively and literally) with a wide range of gangland enforcers, grifters and chancers, and I've investigated crimes so gruesome that I wanted to soak my brain in bleach afterwards.

But I wasn't getting any of those warning signs from the young woman sat opposite me. She seemed naïve, confused, and... nice. I could see why Samson had taken a shine to her.

It was against my better judgement, and liable to lead nowhere, but the fact that she hadn't arrived attached to a name tag was unusual enough to get my attention. As far as I knew, everyone turned up with one.

"So, let me get this straight – you want me to find out where you came from?" I asked.

"Yes, Mr Judas. I do... and what I'm doing here. I'm sure you hear this all the time, but I don't belong here. I don't know how or why, but I know for sure that I shouldn't be... wherever this is."

***

I should have turned her down. Like I said, it's not the kind of case I take on. For a start, no-one knows how anybody ends up in the City. Lots of people have tried, sending them down a one-way spiral that never ends well. I guess it's a natural human drive, the need to know where we come from, and that doesn't go away just because you wake up in Purgatory.

Oddly fascinating as my recent visitor was, there were bills to pay and regular clients to keep happy, and unfortunately for me, this wasn't turning out to be a great week. The Wrath Daemon had completely messed up my investigations into the extra-curricular activities of Mrs Creech, which meant I was going to have to go back to my client and ask for a little more time.

CHAPTER 4

Augustus Creech was much as I had imagined him to be from the name. If you took a vulture and stuck it into a human costume a couple of sizes too big, letting the whole thing sag and crease, that's pretty much what he looked like. Like most of the residents who'd got rich and old in the City, in addition to his appearance, he also shared a few other personality traits with carrion, eagerly feeding off the misfortunes of his fellow man without a second thought.

Also, like most of the older residents with a long history of low-grade nastiness, he had a slightly hunted look about him, an underlying unsatiated hunger, despite his wealth and power. When he slept at night, which, from the dark bags under even darker eyes, seemed like it was rarely, I imagine his dreams were filled with visions of the great Elevator at the centre of the City calling his name. He knew his reckoning was coming.

They say that having nothing to lose makes you dangerous. I disagree, I've had nothing to lose for years and all it means is no-one, other than one very bad-tempered cat, will notice when I'm gone. Mr Creech, on the other hand, had plenty to lose and that meant he would fight with every last breath of his scrawny body, spend every single dollar of his bloated bank account, and plumb the depths of the very darkest corners of his soul, to cling on to what he still had by his dirty, bloodied fingernails.

One of the things he was particularly keen to keep hold of was the latest Mrs Creech. Pretty, ambitious, and unconvincingly breathless in conversation. I had spotted her in Mrs Jones' Club a couple of times before she had ended up with Creech and

I am sure that she's an awful lot smarter than she lets on. Back then she had dark, shoulder-length hair and her own lips. She had worked the bar, not on the barkeep side, but mixed in with the punters, circulating like a butterfly hoovering up the nectar from the willing suckers, each imagining for a moment that their luck had finally turned.

I knew that she was playing them, getting them to pony up the cash for fancy cocktails or bottles of champagne they could scarcely afford. I suppose that made them victims, but on the other hand, for a moment or two they got to feel special, given hope that they had somehow snared the exotic beauty giggling at their tired old jokes. Overall, it didn't seem like that much of a bad deal.

Luckily for me, I was neither rich nor good-looking enough to register as anything other than background noise. It had meant that a couple of times I got to hold a proper conversation with her, when she was taking a break sat at the bar, looking around for the next mark. During those brief, unshielded moments she gave me a window into a young soul that was already tired of this new life.

"Look at him," she muttered to me, on what must have been the fourth or fifth time we ended up sat at the bar as the evening ticked along its slow journey towards the morning.

The 'him' in question was a middle-aged businessman. He was wearing a decent, but not overly expensive, suit, collar undone, tie loose around a slim, pasty, turkey neck. He had the look of a guy who'd been dragged out for one unwilling drink after work and had developed a sudden taste for it, staying on well after his colleagues had called time. There was a definite sway to his steps, and the way he kept one hand against the wall as he walked suggested that, without doing so, he would be struggling to keep his feet.

"You'd think people like him would learn after a while, this city isn't built for them." She broke off with a sigh, and I realised that she wasn't even talking to me anymore. Whatever she was saying wasn't meant for anyone but herself.

It didn't stop her from downing what was left of her drink and walking across to him, her steps becoming increasingly unsteady as she crossed the room. If I hadn't seen the transformation from sober introspection to drunken party girl for myself, all within a matter of a few paces, I would have believed she was every bit as wasted as he was.

The sound of her laughter from across the room, as 'turkey neck' bathed in the momentary glory of her attention, grated on my nerves more than normal. Rather than watch the rest of the scene play out, I headed home, leaving the last of my drink unfinished.

It had been less than a month afterwards that she'd left her job at the club, and another couple of months more before she first appeared on Creech's arm, newly blonde and pouty. I guess she had been staring into the abyss that evening in the club, deciding between the limited options the City was offering her.

I hoped for her sake that she had made the right choice. Frankly, the thought of her bumping uglies with Creech for any amount of money, influence or comfort left me with an overwhelming taste of vomit in my throat. But who am I to judge, the last woman I lost my head over turned out to be worse news than a whole theme park full of Daemons.

As I pulled up outside Creech's place in the well-heeled suburbs outside the centre of the City, the extent of the money and privilege that she had worked her way into was clear. Everything from the wide, open avenues and boulevards of well-maintained trees, to the high gated walls that kept each dwelling safe and sound in a little bubble of privilege, smacked of power, wealth, and a general disdain for the rest of the world.

Don't get me wrong, I don't like the rest of humanity either. I've met enough of them to know that most people are either pointless or horrible. It's just that I don't have the money for things like walls and gates. The closest I can manage is the warm, fuzzy barrier of alcohol and indifference, which seems like a pretty weak alternative to personal security guards and an indoor pool.

The door to Creech manor was designed to be imposing, doing an excellent job of splitting the world in two. There was the bit behind the door and then the rest. It also strongly implied that the bit inside was nicer, with a couple of narrow glass windows that didn't give too much away, just teasing glimpses of a marbled hallway and sweeping staircase.

Perhaps I should have gone to the tradesman's entrance, but I've never let the conventions of class bother me, and I felt a pleasant thrill from dinging the doorbell far more vigorously than necessary. I could hear the measured walk of the housekeeper increasing to a slightly panicked scamper when she realised I was just going to keep ringing until she let me in.

To her credit, she still paused on reaching the door, and hardly glared at all when she slowly pulled it open. This one was a variant on the strict-looking governess model, hair tied back so tightly that if she sneezed it was likely her face would crack. She didn't say anything, just gave me the chilly, superior stare that comes naturally to butlers, housekeepers and nannies. I guess looking down on people helps them come to terms with the fact that they make their living wiping the arse and massaging the ego of some rich, chinless monstrosity or their equally awful offspring.

"Patrick Judas," I volunteered, giving her my most winning smile. It didn't do much to defrost her, although she did look like she might have gagged slightly, albeit in a very refined and minimalist way.

"Mr Creech is expecting you," she finally admitted, although I could tell the whole thing was a bit of a struggle for her. Her eyes kept drifting down to look at the latest bloodstained rips in my jacket. Perhaps it would have been a good idea to change my jacket, or at least get it dry-cleaned to remove the worst of the stains, but I felt it added some credibility to my story about the fight with the Wrath Daemon.... plus, it's the only one I have.

"If you would please follow me?"

The walk through the hallway and up the stairs to Creech's office was an interesting experience. The housekeeper, who had declined to give me her name, was torn between leading the way and trying to keep an eye on me. I think she was worried that I might somehow slip one of the paintings or other pieces of hugely expensive art into my pocket. It meant that she had to keep finding reasons to circle back and check up on me, not helped by the fact that I had decided to take my sweet time, enjoy the ambience, and generally make her life difficult.

The stairway was a curved, sweeping affair that took up loads of space and achieved very little other than making getting up and down stairs take longer than it should. At Creech's age, I would have resented those lost seconds each day.

My unwilling hostess paused in front of the third doorway on the first floor and knocked once.

"Come."

The voice from within was as grand and overblown as the rest of the house. It was the voice of someone very used to being listened to, with the need for politeness or charm left behind long ago.

The Housekeeper turned the handle and pushed the door half open, before taking one step back and gesturing for me to enter.

"It's been a pleasure," I told her with admirable sincerity, as I made my way past.

There was no answer, although she may have winced.

In much the same way as I had managed to picture Creech purely from his name, I was similarly unsurprised by exactly how close his study was to the smoky, wood-panelled cliché that I had imagined. It seemed like Creech had researched what sort of décor an elderly, rich, and horribly corrupt old leech would typically go for, and then ticked off every single item on the list.

One wall was lined with a heavy wooden bookcase, full of expensive leather-bound volumes. They were far too well-ordered and pristine to have ever been read, but they looked the part and were probably worth more than all my worldly goods combined.

The wall opposite was more sparsely, but no less expensively, decorated. The centrepiece was a large oil painting depicting the city at night, spots of red and yellow spattered across a dark, brooding landscape. It was a view that I recognised only too well, looking down from the old hospital, the first thing that any new arrival would see.

Sat precisely midway between the two walls, like a grumpy old thorn wedged uncomfortably between two roses, was the reason I'd dragged my exhausted carcass halfway across the City. Perched behind his desk and favouring me with a look so withering I could feel myself physically ageing under its influence, Creech looked more like a bird of prey than ever. The lighting in the room was set to low and moody, leaving his heavily hooded eyes almost invisible, cast into deep shadow. He hadn't spoken yet, but one wrinkled finger was tapping an impatient beat on the surface of his desk, so I was guessing he wasn't delighted to see me.

I had only been granted an audience once before, it not being hugely discreet to turn up at the house of the woman I had been hired to tail. Creech had fobbed off the staff with a fabricated cover story that I was helping him with some minor corporate espionage. I suppose I looked too disreputable to be convincing as anything more glamorous, and not smart enough to be anything more professional. Like all the best lies, it was ninety per cent true and had been the first indication of the way Creech liked to work.

He prided himself on his old-fashioned sensibilities, which, in his very specific definition of the term, meant unquestioning loyalty and obedience from anyone lucky enough to be taken into his employment. He also liked to keep things simple, hence the straightforward cover story about my employment.

"Give a man enough rope and he'll hang himself," he had told me at the end of our previous meeting, which had been his none-too-subtle way of telling me that he expected me to keep things simple, too.

"Go on then, Mr Judas. Make your excuses and then we can agree how you are going to make it up to me."

I didn't let my surprise show. Frankly, I wasn't all that shocked. In the City, knowledge is power, and Creech had plenty of both. So, the fact that he already knew why I was paying him a house call wasn't all that surprising either.

He didn't look up as I explained about the Wrath Daemon, even when I got to the really good bits. He just kept tapping his finger on the desk like he was counting time.

"I see," he said finally, after leaving a suitably uncomfortable pause at the end of my explanation. "So, what you're telling me is that you don't have the evidence you were hired to provide. I presume you aren't here to ask for more money. I pay for results, Mr Judas, and you haven't provided any."

I hadn't expected anything different, and besides, that wasn't why I was here, although a little surprise about the Daemon would have been nice. Most of the population don't know they exist, but Creech hadn't even blinked.

"I don't need more money, just a little more time."

If he was exasperated, he didn't show it. I suspected that if I really disappointed someone like Creech, then he had more imaginative ways of expressing his displeasure than a few harsh words.

"One more week, Mr Judas. After which, you can consider your employment terminated – one way or another."

"Nice," I thought to myself. About as thinly veiled as a threat could be without actually pointing a gun at my head, but said in a voice so cold and disinterested that I wondered if Creech even cared what my investigations might uncover. He didn't seem like a man given to overwhelming passions, or any sort of emotion other than hunger.

Still, I sucked it up and just nodded once in acknowledgement. He might have all the wealth and power in the world, but his time in the City was drawing to a close and the elevator would take him in the end. If I'm any judge of character, I doubt that Creech was going to like where he was headed next, so if he wanted to be a condescending dick to me now, I could cope with it.

He didn't say anything else, but I heard the study door creak open behind me, which I took as a sign that my audience was over.

CHAPTER 5

"So, how did it go with our charming benefactor?" Samson asked as I slouched back into the office, shaking the rain off my jacket like a damp dog.

"Wonderful," I growled. "He was as pleasant as ever, making it pretty clear that failure to deliver will result in 'unpleasantness'."

"Bloody hell, Judas," Samson scowled at me. "This was supposed to be an easy money job. Follow Mrs Creech around for a bit, prove one way or another if she's being a loving, devoted wife, get paid, and then piss off. 'Unpleasantness' wasn't supposed to come into it."

Pointedly turning his back on me, he stalked off towards his bowl, muttering something under his breath about being "too old for this." Which, by the way, is a load of crap. As far as I can tell, he's no older than me, even when you take cat years into account.

I didn't bother following him. I've known Samson quite long enough to realise that it wouldn't help in the least. Like all cats, he was prone to being over dramatic, so the best thing to do was to leave him to simmer down in his own time.

Instead, I sat down at my desk, leant back, and tried to set my thoughts in order, although I could still see Samson angrily padding around his bed in small stroppy circles.

Like I said earlier, there aren't all that many sentient animals in the City, so I guess the fact that I share an office with one could be considered kinda lucky. Opinion on the matter is split fifty-fifty. Samson thinks I'm lucky. I don't.

It's not like I planned it – it just seemed as if fate had decided that, while I would consistently fail to get a long-term human partner, I was destined to end up with a grumpy feline sidekick.

When I first bumped into Samson, I had been in the City long enough for a talking cat to no longer surprise me, although the circumstances of our meeting should have warned me that he was going to be a handful.

I'd just picked up a new client and had been on a stake-out for hours. The litre of coffee I'd drunk had done a good job keeping me awake but was just starting to knock on the door of my bladder, demanding an immediate exit. I knew I should have planned ahead and rationed myself, but good coffee is one of the very few pleasures in my life. If it was the choice of sitting in my car for hours drinking coffee or whisky, coffee had felt like the more responsible option.

My client for the stakeout, Julius Kerr, was an elderly lawyer with a much younger lover about whom he was starting to have serious doubts. Years of patiently building watertight cases, waiting until he had compiled all the evidence needed before making a move, had led to the old coot carefully planning for his inevitable heartbreak in much the same way.

I had been following his partner for the last three weeks. Once or twice a week he would make some excuse to cancel a planned meeting or dinner, my client would call me up, and if I could get across town in time, then I would do the whole gum-shoe thing. Keeping to a discreet distance, I would follow his lover to whatever rendezvous he had planned, and then report back with times, dates, and photos.

This time I had tailed him to one of the murkier corners of the City, a charming – although thoroughly rotten – corner known as Old Town. They say that this was the first place to be built when the City became... whatever the hell it is now.

It's not true. I know at least one spot that's even older, but it's easy enough to see why people think it.

Same as everything else, things in the City change, evolve. Once upon a time, I guess this would have all been mud huts and before that, caves and the open sky, but for the time being, the City seemed to have settled on skyscrapers, darkened alleyways, neon, and smoke.

Old Town may have lacked the scale and grandeur of the central districts, its brick and stone buildings squat and hunched by comparison, but it made up for that in personality.

You could feel the atmosphere wrapping itself around you as soon as you crossed the boundary, winding its way around your arms and legs, crawling down into your lungs. The further you get into the place, the narrower the streets become, full of derelict building frontages with boarded-up doorways and smashed-in windows, like the eyes and mouths of sad faces mourning their lost past, trying to remember better times, back in the days when they were still beautiful.

The hotel I had ended up outside was one of the better ones. If you risked a quick look above the ground floor you could see signs of the class it had once enjoyed. The casement windows were unbroken, with a series of stepped parapets. Now it just looked like the whole building was recoiling in disgust, pulling itself away from the squalor of the streets below.

Even now, there were a few lingering pretensions of grandeur, the sign outside proudly announcing you could pay for a whole night's stay if you were feeling fancy. You might not wake up with quite as many kidneys as you had on arrival, but at least you'd get a half-decent breakfast in the morning.

There had been no movement at the hotel since I'd arrived, although I was sure there would be plenty going on inside. But this was a strict 'follow and report back' job, which meant no making myself known, and no entering the building. The downside of having been around for so long was that I was getting famous, recognised by pretty much every hotel receptionist, bellhop, bartender and professional escort in the City.

I wasn't sure what the deal was between my client and his squeeze, and I wasn't about to ask. Firstly, it was client privilege. I only ever asked people to share what they wanted to share, or what I needed to get the job done. That tended to be safer for everyone involved and seemed like the vaguely professional thing to do. Secondly, I didn't give even the tiniest of shits.

I know I shouldn't jump to conclusions, and perhaps I should try to have a little more trust in the course of true love, but my guess was that some financial benefit or other was woven into the relationship.

My client, while doing pretty well for himself on the professional front, was not a handsome man, and gave no indication that he had ever been one. Nor did he come across as having a sparkling personality, or any other major positive character traits, unless you counted thoroughness, patience, and excellent knowledge of tax laws.

Sometimes when I have an elderly client, which I do more often than not in this kind of case, you can see the person they used to be, just distorted slightly through the lens of time. You can pick out the ones who have grown old gracefully and those who have fought every step of the way – the ones who willingly pay out for the latest fashionable treatment or procedure in a futile attempt to put a minor speedhump in the inevitable path of age.

Mr Kerr wasn't so vain as to have tried any of that and, to be frank, he would have been throwing his money away. Years of sitting in darkened rooms poring over old legal documents had given him the grey, washed-out look of the recently deceased, which was only exacerbated by a high forehead above which wispy strands of pale hair were plastered haphazardly across the remainder of an unusually large scalp.

By contrast, his young lover was Hollywood good-looking, fine-featured, and almost disgustingly symmetrical. When he smiled, his pearly whites were perfect and looked very expensive, which I guess is why he smiled so much. If you're going to invest in something, you want to show it off as much as possible.

Whatever the deal was, true love or financial convenience, Kerr was in deep enough to have hired me.

It had brought me right across the City, all the way from the reputable suburbs of the west to the shamelessly disreputable fringes of Old Town, sat in a rust-bucket of a car outside a crappy pay-by-the-hour hotel, trying not to piss myself. Sometimes the glamour of my job is almost too much to handle.

The only thing that could have made the situation worse was if a huge cat had suddenly burst through the passenger window of the car, screaming "drive, you stupid bastard," before attaching itself to my leg with inch-long claws… which is exactly what happened.

I reacted in the traditional manner, which was to shout in pain and use most of my favourite swear words.

At the same time, I shook my leg and made a concerted effort to pull the cat loose, but its claws were deeply embedded through my trousers and halfway into my leg.

I would have pressed my point further but was distracted by the sound of my rear windscreen shattering, and even more so by the bullet that clipped my arm on its way through to the dashboard, murdering what was possibly the last working eight-track player in the whole of the City.

It was enough for the cat to let go of my leg and drop into the footwell with a startled hiss.

"Hey dickhead, I said drive," it shouted up at me, "otherwise we're both dead!"

There was another gunshot, but this time I was better prepared and managed to duck slightly, meaning the bullet hit a slightly higher part of my arm this time around.

I had plenty of questions, but I was rapidly running out of bits of arm that I could spare, so decided to save them till later.

Shifting the gearstick into reverse I slammed my foot down on the accelerator, catching my new feline visitor a crack to the side of the head... mainly by accident.

Ignoring the pained yowling, mixed in with the most colourful curses I'd heard since I picked a fight with a bar full of angry poets, (which is an interesting tale, but probably best kept for another time), I kept my foot pressed down, spinning the steering wheel so hard that I bounced off the inside of the car door as the old pile of scrap screeched its mechanical displeasure at me.

Now that I had managed to pull off a one-eighty turn, leaving half an inch of my tyres on the street outside the hotel, I was able to see who had been putting holes in my car and taking chunks out of my arm.

There were at least three of them, although fortunately, only one seemed to have brought a gun, which he was currently frantically reloading. The others had gone a bit more old-school, settling for very heavy and solid-looking lengths of pipe. The nearest of the three made a run at the car, swinging the pipe as he did, shattering what was pretty much my only remaining window, the end of it missing my cheek by a fraction before clanging into the metal frame of the off-side door.

Not waiting for the backswing, I grabbed the end of the pipe, which caught my assailant by surprise, his unfortunate reflex being to grip more tightly, rather than let go. Pushing up into first and accelerating hard again, the car leapt forward, dragging my attacker with me before he bounced off the nearest wall. It also took my wing mirror off, but it seemed worth the sacrifice. By this point, there wasn't much of my car left anyway.

There was another gunshot behind me, as the shooter finally managed to reload, and then I was around the corner and racing away from Old Town, towards the relative safety of pretty much anywhere else.

I drove for another five minutes, eventually stopping off at a drive-thru to pick up another coffee, giving the girl working in the serving hatch my most innocent smile as I handed her the cash through the broken and bloodied shards of my window. It says something about the type of clientele they get late at night that she didn't even blink.

I pulled up in the small car park outside, tried the eight-track which just hissed and sparked, and took a slug of the coffee. It was pretty horrible. Almost tasteless, and yet still so strong that I could feel the lining of my stomach slowly dissolving.

A couple of minutes passed, which I spent binding up the wound in my arm as well as I could, the content of the first aid kit I kept in the glove box more or less rising to the occasion. It would have been more sensible to have gone to the hospital and get professional treatment, leaving the coffee until later, but you know... priorities.

"Right," I said, pausing to take another sip, "I think we need to talk."

"Fine." The voice came from under the driver's seat, where my guest had somehow managed to squeeze himself, despite appearing to be much bigger than the space available, "but I don't think you're going to like it."

It turned out that Samson, as he introduced himself, had been unlucky enough to witness a 'glimmer' deal gone bad. He probably would have been fine, perched on a wall high above the action, but had given himself away with a furious yowl when he had got caught by a random blood splatter.

"If they've got your number plate, they'll be coming for you," he told me, by this point sat on the passenger seat, trying to lick his fur clean. He wasn't enjoying the experience, a look of distaste on his face, making the occasional retching sound when his tongue found a particularly matted patch.

"No need to worry," I replied, pressing the boot release, before getting out and stretching my legs. Rummaging around I pulled out a new set of plates and within a couple of minutes had swapped them out for the previous ones, which I consigned to a bin on the edge of the car park.

It's one of the perks of the work I do. If I'm following someone, on a stakeout, or generally using my car for any business related to my job, I always use substitute number plates. The last thing I want is my work following me home. I'm a bit of a hypocrite like that, happy to follow some poor shmuck for days, but not so keen on them following me.

Of course, all the gang had to do was look out for the shittiest car in the City, but that was a problem for another day.

I don't know why I didn't kick Samson out of my car there and then, but for some inexplicable reason, I let him stay. Maybe the sight of him gagging as he tried to remove a chunk of brain from his fur triggered some sort of long-buried sympathetic reaction, or maybe it was the fact that I hadn't talked to anyone for weeks and he seemed like a good listener. Looking back, I'm pretty convinced that it was a combination of light-headedness and blood loss that affected my judgement, although Samson always goes with the 'good listener' thing.

Anyway, that was more years ago than I care to remember, and Samson's still mooching around the office like he runs the place. The gang never did catch up with us, or at least if they're planning on it, they are taking their sweet time, but Samson never quite got round to leaving. I'm also not sure how he's managed to live quite so long, and he's never felt the need to explain.

In case you're wondering what happened with the case I'd been working, I reported back to Kerr the next day, but left out the whole talking cat and gangland battle part of the story. He seemed a bit too strait-laced for that kind of thing.

He didn't react when I told him where I had found his young lover, just gave a broken nod and sent me on my way.

I only saw him one more time, about a week later when I went to his office to pick up my final pay cheque. The photo of his partner was gone from his desk, but when he pulled open the top drawer to get his cheque-book, I could have sworn I saw a small plastic bag full of glistening, pearly-white teeth.

CHAPTER 6

Samson was still in a foul mood, and Mrs Creech was spending the afternoon with dear old hubby, so I decided to use my free time to do some digging. Specifically, I wanted to see what I could uncover about my nameless visitor from earlier that day. Something about her story had got under my skin and was itching away uncomfortably, so I decided to pay a visit to City Hall.

It was one of the oldest buildings in the centre of the City. Not quite as ancient as the huge, sharp office block that held the Elevator, although it looked far older. The whole place was formed of huge stone blocks, with heavy lintels and tall, slim windows that glared out suspiciously at the surrounding streets. Crouched among the steel and glass skyscrapers that surrounded it, the building remained squat, grumpy, and resolutely unchanged.

It had been a while since I last visited. My line of work tends to rub some people up the wrong way, and something in my character means I normally end up making things worse, even when I don't need to. I might not be able to do much about being stuck in this damn place, but it doesn't mean I can't stick two fingers up at the establishment now and then.

Unfortunately for me, pretty much anyone with influence or leverage has a line of some sort straight back to the rogue's gallery that runs City Hall, which means I have earned myself a pretty permanent spot on the 'not welcome' list.

The City is ruled by an elected group of three who operate out of the building, generally referred to by anyone safely out of earshot as the 'unholy trinity'. When I say elected, everyone assumes that's how they land the top jobs. While the people sitting at the top table might change now and then, I don't recall there ever being an actual election, and I've been here a long, long time.

Law and order currently falls to Police Chief Harland. A tall, predatory looking woman with all the charm of an angry raptor, and the moral code to match. She's the reason that most of Old Town is a lawless free-for-all, that the sale of 'Glimmer' is going through the roof, and why anyone in genuine need seems to be coming to me for help rather than trying the police. She could scrub her fingers until they were bloody stumps and her hands would still be dirty.

She's also extremely smart and totally ruthless. The last person to openly challenge her for the job ended up nailed inside a box in Old Town harbour, in the world's most unlikely suicide.

The day-to-day running of the City is managed by our glorious leader, Mayor Eric Hunter. A short, squat man with all the charisma of an open sore, he has made a career based upon never taking risks, never expressing an opinion, and never wearing anything other than a nondescript grey suit.

It has served him well. He's been in post longer than any mayor I can remember, and I've outlasted a few. I'm pretty sure that somewhere beneath that bland exterior beats the heart of a true psychopath. The whole façade of greyness is just too perfect, too complete, to be anything other than a smokescreen. Whatever he is, to keep someone like Harland on such a tight leash, there has to be some hidden strength within the guy.

The final member of their select little group is responsible for the administration of justice and is also the newest of the three, Mason Grieve. I haven't figured him out yet, other than the fact that he seems ambitious as hell and likes nice suits. He's also either extremely young for a Chief Justice or has the number of a very good plastic surgeon. Although he's still fresh in post, it's hard to get away from him. His good looks and an ability to string more than two words together have led to a constant carousel of interviews and television appearances.

He popped up out of nowhere when the previous Senior Judge retired due to an unfortunate case of being dead, after one too many attempts to shake down one of the local crime lords.

Being a corrupt old bastard goes with the territory, but it also comes with a number of unwritten ground rules, which include not overstepping your boundaries. If you do, then no matter who you are, it's only a matter of time until you could expect a gentle tap on the shoulder. If you were lucky, that's all it would be, just a delicate, whispered reminder that you needed to behave yourself. If you weren't, or you had pushed your luck one too many times, then it would be the second-to-last thing you would ever feel.

***

I've felt that dreaded tap on my shoulder once, not long after my arrival, and before my ideals had been completely eroded by the rough tides of experience.

I'd been hired by a young woman called Katya, an employee of one of the more successful local businesses. She wanted help fighting an unfair dismissal case after questioning a few of the company's working practices and being shown the door for her efforts. I'm no lawyer, but evidence that her claims had some basis would help when it came to court. It wasn't a big job, and my client hadn't got all that much cash to throw at it.

She had cleaned out her savings. A few of her former co-workers, while not having the moral conviction to actually stick their necks on the line, had also put a little money into her meagre battle chest, enough to fund a couple of weeks of my time.

She wasn't a typical client, who tended to be at the older and wealthier end of the spectrum. Instead, she was young, with a nervous smile that would pop to the surface unexpectedly halfway through a sentence, as if she felt the constant need to apologise for her words. She had a broad face, dotted with freckles that would dance with each brief smile, and a habit of pausing whenever she had to say anything bad or unpleasant, the words not coming naturally to her. I liked her immediately, which I guess is why I took the case. That, and the fact that I needed the money.

A week after I started my investigations, which had been making slow but steady progress, I was on my way back to the office after a couple of drinks when I felt a stirring in the air behind me.

Even back then I had a natural sense for trouble, and knowing whoever it was had got so close without triggering any sort of warning meant they were pretty good at their job.

Before I could turn, a heavy hand dropped onto my shoulder and held it in place, with the strong implication that turning around would not be encouraged. When he spoke, the voice behind me was wavering and uneven, hardly intimidating, yet so unusual that I was filled with more unease than I could explain.

"You have been poking around in private business, Mr Judas."

The hand on my shoulder squeezed for emphasis. Whoever it was had decided they really wanted to hammer the point home, the fingers pressing into my flesh until I heard an unpleasant popping sound. It was accompanied by a flash of darkness across my vision, illuminated by sharp little shards of pain. Imagine fireworks dancing across your eyes, but with the prettiness offset by really horrible pain.

"Consider this a warning. You make sure to be a good boy from now on, otherwise we will be chatting again."

There was another squeeze, even harder this time. It was enough to bring me to my knees, trying not to vomit as my shoulder decided it was time to share its pain with the rest of my body.

Then the hand was gone, the pressure released, light footsteps tapping off into the distance. After a few minutes, I got myself together enough to lurch back on to my feet, where I finally caved in and threw up. Realising that I had pushed myself too far with the whole standing up thing, I sat down again and had a good long rest, waiting for the pain to drop to just about bearable. Eventually, I was able to stagger the rest of the distance back to the office, swallow about a kilo of painkillers, and try to get some sleep.

I hadn't realised at the time just how lucky I was. It had been the first, although sadly not the last time I'd cross paths with the owner of that creepy, wavering voice.

I'm not the only one who's been stuck in this place longer than normal. After making a few enquiries I found out that the heavy hand had belonged to a gangland enforcer called Cain. That fleeting moment was the start of a long and complicated relationship, mainly consisting of him trying to kill me or one of my clients, and me trying to stop him.

It's fair to say we don't get on.

The following morning the news reported on the latest grim findings down at the docks. The body of a young woman found in the shallow mud, currently unidentified. I didn't need to look at the blurred image for more than a moment to recognise the broad, freckled face, and to know I wouldn't be seeing that pretty, nervous smile lighting it up ever again.

A better man would have gone to the police, shared what he knew, or at least suspected. A better man would have tried to get some sort of justice. But I didn't do either of those things. I just shut down the case, pocketed the money that I had been paid, and tried not to think about Katya and the times she had sat there in my office, smiling shyly and struggling to say anything bad about the bastards who would end up killing her.

Anyway, I digress. The point I was trying to make, in such a roundabout way, is that the people who run the City are not nice, and asking for any kind of help at City Hall was just as likely to drop me into a world of trouble as it was to assist my investigations. If I had a choice, I would stay well away from the place, but unfortunately there are a few things that only City Hall and the lovable public servants who inhabit the building can provide, and Arrival Certificates are one of those things. It's basically a Birth Certificate, but without the birth part. Even if the young woman who had asked for my help didn't know what her name was, chances are there would be a record of her arrival buried somewhere in the archives, which would at least give me something to work with.

The approach to the front doors, leading to the main reception foyer, was designed to be imposing, and for the most part it worked. Keeping with the heavy stone motif, the surround to the open doorway was decorated with the carved busts of ancient sword-wielding warriors dispensing justice and defending the down-trodden. It was all very inspiring but bears no relation to the actual function of City Hall, which is to tread as heavily as possible on the already down-trodden and to only dispense justice in exchange for cash, privilege, and a designated parking space.

It was a quiet day, and the foyer was almost completely empty. There were just a couple of bored-looking security guards, an elderly lady who was berating one of the long-suffering clerks, and a handful of other office staff, who were pointedly ignoring the fate of their beleaguered colleague. I was pretty sure I recognised the old woman from the last time I had visited, she had been pretty angry back then too, with a face that was naturally set to 'disapproving'. I guess this might just be the way she chose to pass the time. Some people drink, some watch TV, I suppose she liked to verbally abuse public officials. At least it's free and gets her out of the house.

"How can I help you today?"

41

The clerk behind the counter was new, or at least I presumed she was, as her disgustingly perky greeting sounded like it was at least fifty percent genuine.

Fighting my natural urge to growl, retch, or make some other entirely inappropriate response to what was, essentially, a friendly greeting, I twisted my face into a reasonable facsimile of a smile. In addition to the lack of sincerity, my attempt was further undermined by the fact that I hadn't yet fully recovered from having my face half-melted, cut, grazed, and pummelled over the last few days. The clerk blanched a little but bounced back with commendable enthusiasm.

"Lovely weather for the time of the year," she said, still fizzing with the misplaced bonhomie of someone who thought I cared.

"Lovely," I agreed, whilst pointedly wiping the damp from the sleeve of my coat. I tried smiling again, although dialling it back a bit, to see if the end result was any less terrifying. It seemed like a good idea to stay civil. At least someone new and keen might help me out, with the added bonus that she probably didn't know who I was.

"I'm looking for some records," I added. "I work for Friendly Mountain Insurance and need to check out someone's Arrival Certificate." I flashed my wallet quickly, the fake ID proudly proclaiming me to be a registered Insurance Investigator.

The Clerk, whose rather more legitimate badge identified her as Diana, and also as someone who was 'here to help', looked down at her screen and clattered away on the keyboard, hammering the keys with the same enthusiasm she seemed to apply to all aspects of her work.

"Hmmm. You'll need to go down to Public Records for that," she said. "If you take the lift or stairs down to basement Level One, you should find what you need."

She tapped a few more keys.

"And you'll need a temporary pass, Mr...?

She left a polite gap for me to fill.

"Samson," I replied, crossing my fingers behind my back.

"Here you go, Mr Samson", she smiled back, handing me a small laminated pass. "Now, you have a wonderful afternoon."

Wondering if it was possible for my ears to get diabetes, I headed towards the stairs, waving my pass at the nearest security guy, who was disinterested to a post-graduate level. I was fairly sure the pass could have proclaimed me to be a professional murderer, arsonist and tax dodger, and he would still have let me through.

'Records' was pretty much as you might imagine – a library, but with all the good bits taken out. There were a few old computer terminals that had been out of order every time I visited, a couple of ancient microfiche readers, and a mass of old bookcases filled with files, boxes, and dust. It didn't seem to matter how recent the records were, you could have someone arrive in the City a few days ago, and their file would still look like it had been dug up with the Pharaohs.

I didn't have a huge amount to go on, but if what my visitor had told me was correct, then she had arrived somewhere between two and three days ago. During my previous visits to the archives, I had gained a passing familiarity with the place, so it didn't take too long to find the ledger I was looking for and lug it across to the nearest free desk. It looked more like an ancient tome of dark magic than an official record, but when I flicked the heavy pages over to check out the most recent entries, the inside was filled with nothing more exciting than a neat list of names, times, and dates.

Looking at the list, I felt a jolt of excitement. It seemed that luck was on my side for once, with only a handful of names recorded as arrivals in the last three days. My visitor hadn't seemed like an 'Albert', 'Nathaniel', or 'Brett', which left me with just two to choose from. Presuming that she had been recorded in the arrival's ledger, my guest was either 'Deborah' or 'Eve'.

I was just closing the ledger when I noticed a slight mark on the edge of the page, an inky smudge as if someone had licked their finger before turning the page. I don't know why it stood out to me – it's not like I had a monopoly on flicking through old records, but it looked recent and, whatever the reason, logical or not, I could feel the hairs on my arms tingling.

CHAPTER 7

I wasn't quite ready to go back to the office and be glared at by Samson, so I decided to go and see Father Trent instead. He's about the closest thing I have to a friend, if you ignore grumpy felines.

We hadn't planned to meet up, so I gave him a quick call just to make sure he was free, although I needn't have bothered. Pretty much any time of the day or night, he was only likely to be in one place. It was one of the few advantages of having a priest for a friend. That, and the free crackers.

He probably has a first name, but I've always called him Trent, and he's never volunteered anything further. The way names get handed out in this place it could be something like Goliath, or even worse. The kind of name that would make being taken seriously as a priest in the middle of Purgatory a trickier sell than it already was.

If you think I've seen some bad things, that's nothing compared to what Father Trent has to deal with every single day. Believe me when I tell you, taking confession in a city like this is no picnic. He never shares what people tell him, but from the look on his pale face, damp with sweat when he finally makes his way out, some of it must be seriously horrible stuff.

We tend to come at things from the opposite end of the spectrum. Father Trent somehow still believes there's good in each of us, and me... well, I've seen enough to know that most of the characters in this place have enough darkness in the corners of their souls to submerge the whole city if it ever leaked out. But, despite our fundamental disagreement over the goodness of mankind, we have always got along.

Part of it comes down to the fact that we've both been here a long time, and part of it's just that he's a good man, or at least as good as you'll find in the City.

Ever since I first met him, Father Trent has spent most of his time deep in the recesses of the City's only church. Right on the boundary of Old Town and the central district, uncomfortably straddling the two, it had become a rather jaded symbol of forgotten hope. When Father Trent first arrived and decided to take the place on, it had been little more than an abandoned stone shell. A dusty old frame waiting for a canvas to fill it.

It had taken time, patience, and more backbone than I gave him credit for, but slowly Father Trent had breathed life back into the place. The congregation had grown in dribs and drabs, a few desperate characters to begin with, thinking it couldn't do their chances any harm, then a few more, week after week, adding to the numbers. There were even a couple of keen volunteer 'Curates' who you would generally find fussing around the place and who'd helped Trent repair, replace, and replenish. I was pretty sure that one of Trent's helpers in particular had developed a soft spot for him. Either that, or they were naturally given to uncontrollable blushing and stammering whenever they saw a dog collar, which made their current choice of pastime an unfortunate one.

While Trent seemed to be blissfully ignorant of his admirer, and the tangled path of romance in general, one of the very few vices he did allow himself was a decent single malt. He didn't drink to excess, just allowed himself enough to sand the edges off the rough corners of life, and maybe blur the memories of the latest confession he'd had to sit through.

I'm not such a connoisseur, but I can appreciate a good quality whisky in the same way I can appreciate movies. I might generally limit myself to schlocky action movies, full of throwaway dialogue and terribly scripted fight scenes, but when I get the opportunity I can still enjoy the occasional arthouse film or award-winning biopic.

By the time I arrived, he already had two glasses set out on the small table in his 'office'. It wasn't much more than a glorified cubby-hole, but he'd made it comfortable with an assembly of oddly mismatched furniture collected over the years.

"How's life treating you then, Judas?"

He always called me that since our first meeting, which you would think would be a tricky one for a religious man to get his head around. Turns out he finds the whole name thing amusing but decided to keep that fact to himself until we were a good way down the road to being friends.

"Same as always, unpacking the emotional baggage of rich, unpleasant people. How about you?"

"Pretty similar," Trent replied with a smile, although I knew he didn't mean it. Somehow, even after all the terrible things he'd seen and heard, he still couldn't view people in the City as anything other than misguided lost souls. He took a sip of his whisky and gave a contented sigh.

"Not bad, eh? This is a gift from one of my Curates. Said I looked like I needed cheering up."

A slight frown creased his forehead, which had slowly grown over the years I had known him. He still had a dusting of dark hair spread across the back half of his scalp, but it was fighting a losing battle. His habit of nervously running his fingers through his hair had slowly evolved, through necessity, into scratching the back of his neck, which he was subconsciously doing now.

"I don't look that miserable, do I?"

"No more than normal. They probably just wanted an excuse to do something nice," I said, leaving out the codicil that the gift was an unspoken sign of affection, obvious to anyone except Trent.

In truth, he was looking a bit worse for wear, the dark circles under his eyes were heavier than normal and there was an underlying hoarseness to his voice that hinted at restless nights.

I had probably lingered slightly too long with my answer, drawing a tired, accepting smile from my old friend.

"It's fine," he said. "I might not be all that pretty, but I still own a mirror, and recently it's telling me I haven't been sleeping all that well, even if everyone else tries to spare my feelings."

"Anything I can do?"

"I don't think so," Trent replied with a regretful shake of his head. "It's not something that anyone can help with, not even you."

He paused and took a deep, slow inward breath before continuing.

"I've been dreaming," Father Trent admitted, slightly shamefaced. "For the last couple of weeks. It's been the same dream every night. There's an elevator off in the distance, with a bright light shining out between the gap in the doors, brighter than anything I've ever seen."

He stopped to take another sip of his whisky, pausing with the glass halfway to his lips and turning it from side to side, letting the light refract through the cut glass of its heavy base. When he spoke again his voice was distant, a mix of regret and longing threaded through his words.

"The Elevator is calling to me, in my dreams. I try to ignore it, resist it, but every night I get a little bit closer to the doors before I wake up."

I raised my glass and clinked it against the side of his. I could have asked any number of questions, but we both knew where the conversation would end up, and we had been friends long enough to realise it wasn't necessary.

To be honest, I was surprised it had taken this long. For

all the time I had known him, Father Trent had been a rock amongst the shifting sands of the City, an anchor point for lost souls trying to fight the tide. He was a rare thing, a genuinely good man, with no apparent interest in getting himself out of the City and off to somewhere better.

But, good man or not, eventually the Elevator reaches out to each of us, and try as you might, no one can resist its call for long. It's the final arbiter. You can spend your time here however you please. You can be good, bad, or indifferent, with not much outside of crooked cops or the broken-down train-wreck of a legal system to keep you in check, but the Elevator will judge us all in the end.

I didn't doubt that Trent would be going somewhere better. There was no fear in his eyes when he spoke about his dreams, the light he had seen spilling through the doors was a promise, rather than a threat. I was happy for him, but it was still painful to know I would soon be losing his company.

"How about you, Judas?" Trent asked after a couple of minutes. I could tell he wanted to change the subject, so I opened up a little more than I normally would.

"It's been a strange sort of day, to be honest. I have a case, a new one, and it's not like anything I've come across before."

Trent leaned forward a little in his chair. He tended not to be that interested in my work, but for the moment he was keen enough to indulge me and occupy the awkward silence that was threatening to fill the room.

"There was a girl," I began, ignoring Trent's raised eyebrow. He knew me well enough to realise that any story starting with, "there was a girl," was likely to end up with me getting beaten up, drowned or set on fire, rather than any sort of romance.

"She seemed lost, genuinely lost. More so than most people when they end up here. I know it sounds crazy, but I honestly don't think she belongs here. She seemed… innocent."

Trent put down his glass and sat back with a sigh, rubbing his forehead.

"No-one in the City is truly innocent, Judas. Not you, not me, not anyone. We can do our best to make amends, to improve ourselves, but something brought us here in the first place, and it wasn't innocence."

"I know. Like I said… it sounds crazy. Still, something about her got under my skin. I checked her out at City Hall and there were only a couple of possibilities. I just need to trim it down to one, see where it takes me."

"I recognise that look," Trent said. "I've seen it before, and I guess you won't be giving up on this one until you find your answers. If I could offer a word of advice?"

"Sure."

"If you want to find out which of the new arrivals is your mystery girl, I'd start at the beginning."

I nodded, although without any great enthusiasm. I knew he meant the old hospital on the hill, and I suppose it made sense. It's just that the place still gave me the creeps. My arrival in the City didn't hold any fond memories and I've managed to put off going back there ever since. Considering the number of years I've been stuck in this place, that's pretty damn impressive.

"It'll do you good, Judas," Trent said with a smile. "Help you exorcise a few demons of your own."

My response wasn't suitable for a place of worship, so I won't repeat it now.

CHAPTER 8

I left it until the morning before making the drive out to the Hospital. By the time I had finished with Trent, it was getting late and poking around dingy corridors in the murky semi-light of the morning, rather than the complete darkness of the night, was a slightly more tempting prospect.

It was a short journey, although I would have been happy for it to last longer. The flickering neon and dirty brick walls of the City gave way to a largely barren landscape of desert and scrub as I drew closer to my destination.

Despite the drizzle, it gets hellishly hot outside the confines of the City itself, and my car is far too old, cheap, and broken to have any fancy extras like air conditioning, or windows that still open. Consequently, by the time I arrived I was sweating, grumpy, and more on edge than I would like, which is not a great combination for efficient detective work.

Regardless of the prolonged passage of time since I had last set foot inside the Hospital, it was immediately and unpleasantly familiar. If you took a big and scary-looking Gothic building, covered it in a thin veneer of old, crumbly brickwork, smashed most of the windows, and made sure the few that survived were positioned in such a way you could never quite see into them, but still gave the impression that someone was looking out, then you are about half-way to imagining just how creepy the place was.

If I was lucky, I would be able to make my way through to the bowels of the place – the ward where all the new arrivals turned up – give the place a quick search, and then get out before anything major went wrong.

On the other hand, if I was unlucky, I would end up timing my search to coincide with the arrival of one or more new residents, which could get messy.

The main doors of the Hospital were set into a wide, low portico, sticking out from the main building like a protruding lower lip. It didn't help to dispel the feeling that I was entering the mouth of a giant hungry beast. A beast that had already spat me out once. Although the doors were closed, they weren't locked, and the nearest one of the pair swung inwards almost silently when I gave it a tentative push.

The lack of a sinister-sounding creak may have been a little anti-climactic, but the interior of the building didn't disappoint. It was every bit as grubby, dingy and unpleasant as I remembered. The kind of place that would give even the most hardened serial killer a bad case of the heebie-jeebies. Cobwebs hung in thick, gathered clusters from every available surface, making each inhaled breath a risky undertaking.

Oddly, despite the webs, there were no spiders anywhere to be seen. I could only assume that something had been eating them. Either that, or they were all hiding, biding their time...

As I said, this place doesn't hold particularly happy memories for me, and my brain tends to react to stressful situations by going off at unhelpful tangents. The best thing is to press on, avoiding any further distractions, including spider-based conspiracy theories.

The room I needed to access was some way from the entrance, deep in the furthest recesses of the building. Although it had been a lifetime since I had walked, run, or, for a brief time, crawled through the corridors, it was all remarkably familiar. To my right was the long-abandoned reception area, dirty glass partitions still rising above the dark wood of the desk. Frames that had once held posters with health advice or offers for medical insurance were hanging empty on the walls, a few fragments of ripped, yellowing paper all that remained.

Straight ahead was the corridor that led deeper into the hospital and towards the ward where I had arrived, so that was the way I headed, walking straight past one final door, sign-posted 'surgery', which I pointedly ignored.

Just to be clear, there is no way I will ever go through that door. There's creepy and then there is just obviously wrong, and that door was all kinds of wrong.

So, avoiding the distractions to either side, I trudged on in the direction of the wards. They all had beatific, misleading names, like Buttercup or Sunflower, with each one depicted by a scrawled child's painting of the flower in question.

I should mention at this point that there are pretty much zero children in the City. We all arrive as fully grown adults, pre-sumably because a kid generally hasn't done enough bad stuff in their life to merit being sent here. Bearing that fact in mind should make you realise that having kid's drawings on the wall was pretty damn weird.

There was a rattle in the distance, the sound of metal clanking on metal, and the pattering of footsteps. I tensed, my hand creeping unconsciously to the spot where my pistol would normally be nestled, before I remembered I had left it locked away in the office. The hospital might be grim and creepy, but it played an important, almost spiritual role in the City, and bring-ing a gun into the place just hadn't felt like something I should do.

Now I was here, and apparently not alone, I was begin-ning to regret that moment of moral fortitude. Fortunately for all involved, the sound faded, the steps heading away rather than towards me. Still, the potential for bumping into some-thing else alive in the place spurred me on, speeding up my pace and encouraging me to pay attention to my surroundings, rather than getting too wrapped up in my thoughts.

The ward I was looking for was pretty much the last one down the corridor, Foxglove. The illustration was particularly special, a series of pink-purple splodges running down a wonky green stem. The door was open, just far enough for me to see the edge of a couple of unmade hospital beds, but not quite enough to see if someone was in them.

Still, no time like the present. I hadn't heard any more footsteps, but it was only a matter of time before someone or something turned up, so, snapping on my torch, I bravely ventured into the room, hardly shitting myself at all.

It was every bit as horrible as I remembered, although from a slightly different angle, having never entered the room through this door before, only exited. It did, however, seem smaller, just big enough for two rows of four beds nestled against the northern and southern walls. There wasn't much in the way of other furniture or medical apparatus, just a couple of heavy domed metal lights hanging on chains from the ceiling. The bulbs had long since burned themselves out, so the only illumination I had was the slim beam of my flashlight, which skittered across the pitted metal of the light fittings before settling back on the beds.

The first row was a complete washout, revealing nothing other than some very suspect looking sheets. I'm not squeamish, but I expect fabric to bend a little when you lift it.

Turning my attention to the beds lined up against the southern wall, I swept the beam of my flashlight back and forth, hoping for a little more luck. The bedding on one of them looked like it had been disturbed relatively recently, so it was there I focused my attention.

The bed itself was frustratingly empty of any clues, other than a dent in the stained pillow. Crouching down to peer underneath revealed a further mass of spider's webs, even more thickly gathered than those I had passed in the reception... although still no actual spiders.

It meant that the light from my torch was split a thousand times by the interlacing strands of web, making it hard to see much beyond them and casting an impressive set of shadows across the rear wall.

I had pretty much resigned myself to delving deeper, and probably getting a mouthful of cobweb into the bargain, when I caught a glimpse of something. A hard edge that glinted for a moment in the torchlight.

I dropped to the floor, lying prone to get a better look, but before I could see anything more, I was disturbed by the sound of barely audible footsteps a little way off in the distance. I couldn't tell for sure if they were the same as those I'd heard earlier, but it didn't matter. Any footsteps in this place belonged to feet I didn't want to run into. Judging distance in the echoey wards and corridors of the hospital was tricky, but they didn't sound that far away, and they were getting louder.

Cursing under my breath and wishing I had longer arms, I crawled under the bed just far enough to grab whatever it was that I had spotted before. It was small, thin and made of plastic, but that was about all I could tell without taking a proper look.

Scrabbling back out and doing my best not to breathe in, I pushed myself back up onto my feet and took a quick glimpse down. Clutched in my hand, and festooned with hanging threads of web, was a small plastic wristband, a name scrawled inexpertly across it.

'Eve'

Perfect. I gave myself a quick pat on the back. At least I knew the name of my client now, even if she didn't know it herself.

My introspection was shattered by another scurrying sound, closer again than before. It was hard to tell, but what I had first taken to be an echo was now sounding more like several pairs of feet rather than one.

Deciding that I had worn out my welcome, I pushed my way back through the doors to the ward and set off down the corridor at a flat run. It meant that I was making a fair bit of noise, both from the thudding of my feet and the laboured breathing of a man who needs to work on his cardio.

A little way ahead of me, I could see the welcome sight of the hospital's main entrance, the anaemic glow of the morning half-heartedly pushing its way through the dirty glass of the doors. It wasn't enough to bring any light into the building, but at least it gave me something to aim for.

The sound of feet behind me was still there, somewhere over my shoulder, and seemed louder than ever. I tried to find a bit more speed, attempting to tap into any hidden energy reserves I may have held back for emergencies. Unfortunately, it seemed I didn't have any.

Still, I made it to the door before anything unpleasant caught up with me, which was pretty much where the good news ended. The bad news started immediately afterwards, beginning with the sight of my car's two front tyres. Someone had really gone to town on them, reducing them to a few shredded wisps of rubber. This was followed almost immediately by the sound of the heavy doors between the hospital corridor and the reception area clattering open, which meant that whoever had caught my scent was now only a few seconds away.

Cursing my bad luck, my car, and whoever had invented shitty cheap tyres, I set off at a run down the hill towards the distant lights of the City. Or at least, as close to a run as I could manage.

CHAPTER 9

By the time I reached the outskirts of the City, barrelling through the outermost streets of Old Town, I had been alternately running and trying not to puke for about twenty minutes.

More than once I had glimpsed the outline of one of my pursuers in the distance. Whoever they were, they had stayed a pretty consistent distance behind me for the entire journey, making me think they were enjoying themselves and just stringing things out for their own pleasure. Not the most reassuring of thoughts.

I pelted around the corner, skidding on a discarded can, arms and legs flailing wildly, and regaining my balance just in time to bounce off the nearest wall.

Although I know the City pretty well, I'd lost track of my route during the last panicked stages of the chase and managed to find myself in a warren of back alleys that I'd never seen before. That turned out to be a real shame, otherwise I might have realised a bit earlier that I was sprinting towards a dead end.

I think my pursuers knew it. The commotion of their chase had dropped off a bit, the scurry of running feet changing to more measured footsteps. Trying to stay calm, I looked around in the hope of spotting a way out, but there was nothing.

As dead ends go, it was a really good one. High brick walls to both sides, with no windows or doors, not even one of those rickety old metal fire escapes that so often turn up in movies just when you need them. At the far end was a chain-link fence at least twenty feet high, which to my mind seemed excessive. At least it had opened up the claustrophobic narrowness of the alley a little, giving way to what was essentially a small open courtyard.

Tactically, the alleyway was probably better, narrow enough that I could face my pursuers one at a time, but I don't enjoy confined spaces.

The footsteps were getting closer, their steady rhythm echoing off the walls. Trying to slow my breathing and prepare myself for what was coming, I closed my eyes and concentrated on the footsteps. It was tricky, with the sound of several steps overlapping, but I decided there were at least three of them.

Despite the onset of morning, the alleyway was still shrouded in darkness. The City is never light at the best of times, and today had the added inconvenience of a thick fog that had settled across the grey, dismal streets.

As I would definitely rather face my pursuers in the light, I backed up until I was pretty much in the centre of the court-yard, where the illumination from a flickering lamp hanging from the nearest building was just bright enough to pick out most of my surroundings.

Wishing once again that I'd brought my gun – or prefer-ably lots of guns and a group of friends to help carry them – I cast around for other options. I'm sure a regular hero type would have been able to rustle up a length of pipe or something useful, whereas my options were a dustbin or a plant pot, the latter still holding someone's doomed floral attempt to brighten up the place. Deciding not to look a gift horse in the mouth, even if the gift horse on this occasion had no teeth – and was dead – I settled on the bin. Grabbing the lid and clutching it like a shield with one hand, I held it protectively across my chest, focusing my at-tention on the alleyway.

The first of my pursuers to enter the courtyard was small and weedy, with an apologetic slump to his shoulders that didn't match the hungry expression on his face. He was wearing a de-cent suit, but one that had seen better days, or possibly even weeks, the material shiny with damp and disregard.

Two more followed shortly after, none of them individually appearing all that threatening. On another day, on a different street, I would happily have walked past any one of them without a second glance, or perhaps, if I was feeling flush, tossed them a few coins.

The only thing they had in common was an air of neglect, of smart clothes and expensive haircuts gone to wrack and ruin. Closest to me was a young woman, possibly somewhere between twenty and thirty years old, her naturally pretty face apparent underneath the grime. Opening her mouth in a broad smile when she saw me, I got a glimpse of decayed stumps, still stubbornly hanging on to her gums, black and rancid.

The final member of the trio was older, although it was hard to tell his age under the bushy beard that had taken over most of his face. As with the other two, his clothes looked like they had started life somewhere in the business district, the daily outfit of a trader, or banker, or some other fancy word for career criminal. Whoever he was, he had lived well for a while, the pinstripes of the suit not completely camouflaging a generous stomach.

They didn't say anything. Not to me and not to each other, just slowly fanned out across the courtyard, the two younger ones taking up positions on either side of me, and my new friend with the beard straight ahead, making sure there was no chance I could slip past them and back down the alley.

The light above me flickered again, dropping the courtyard into darkness for a split second. As it did so, my three pursuers were dipped in shadow, only their outline remaining. That, and an acidic green glow from the spots where their eyes should be.

"That's just great," I muttered to myself, wishing I had paid more attention to the warning signs earlier.

That explained why they were moving so easily, despite their ragged appearance. My new fan club weren't exactly human, or at least not anymore. It looked like I had managed to seriously annoy someone – someone with enough sway to send three Envy Daemons after me.

You remember the Wrath Daemon. Big, dumb, goes "Raaagh," quite a lot? And you remember I said they weren't the worst? Well, these three were a step up from that. Not quite at the top of the pile when it comes to sheer evil fuckery, but definitely up there.

Envy Daemons get into your head when you feel life is short-changing you. looking at your colleagues across the office, you bitch about the fact that the promotion, the raise, the plaudits, all of it – should be yours, not someone else's.

Most of the time you get over it, move on with your life. But these three were examples of what happens when you don't. When every waking moment is filled with the desire for something more. Eventually, an Envy Daemon will start to whisper in your ear, promising to help you get what you think you're owed.

Their offer is completely genuine, in a way. But it's better to stop and have a good hard think about what you really deserve, before agreeing to their terms.

The three sorry individuals circling me obviously hadn't taken the time to do that, and were now nothing more than a skin bag for their new hosts, the only external signs being the slow deterioration of their disregarded bodies and the tell-tale green glow bleeding out from their eye sockets.

Most common parlance has a grounding in truth somewhere down the line. They don't call envy the 'Green-Eyed Monster' for nothing. It's just that most people have forgotten why. Personally, I prefer 'those parasitic evil little bastards', but 'Green-Eyed Monster' is probably catchier – and easier to teach in Sunday school.

Running into one of them is a problem. They're devious, vicious, and much stronger than the broken shells they inhabit. A group is much worse, a predatory pack of supernatural hyenas.

They enjoy what they do, I know that much. Even at this distance, I could see the cruel smile on the older one's face. The thought of mashing my skull into the pavement was giving him happy chills, and by the high-pitched giggles coming from the other two, I could tell they were feeling it too.

The element of surprise is always important, particularly when you're outnumbered and trapped in a dark alley by a group of demonic assholes with a major grudge, and nothing is more surprising than being charged at, by a scruffy man holding a dustbin lid.

To be fair, it nearly worked. There was a flicker of confusion in the nearest Daemon's expression, which briefly changed to annoyance, and then to unconsciousness as I chucked a load of Magick into the flimsy tin lid before hitting him with it like a battering ram.

That took care of the scrawny one for the moment, although it wouldn't be long before he was up and about again. All I'd done was briefly incapacitate the human host, but the Envy Daemon was still fully conscious and raging that its 'ride' had been temporarily put out of commission.

Unfortunately, that still left the woman with bad dental hygiene and the older gent to deal with.

"You should have stayed away, Mr Judas." The woman rasped, in a voice more full of old malice than any human throat could manage. No wonder her teeth had rotted away, the bile in her words was enough to strip paint.

I couldn't agree more. I really should have kept out of it, whatever 'it' was. Unfortunately, I didn't have a clue.

The bearded Daemon had taken the chance to make up a bit more of the distance between us, his hands clenching and unclenching rhythmically, predicting violence.

Concentrating on him ended up being a mistake. Taking advantage of my temporary distraction, his companion rushed me from the side, grabbing my arm with claw-like strength before I could yank myself clear. I turned and struck her cleanly on the nose with my free hand, which gave an unpleasant popping sound as the bone broke.

It didn't achieve much, although she did open her mouth to give a hiss of displeasure. I could feel the acidic burn of her breath wafting over my shoulder, harsh enough to sting my skin and bring tears to my eyes.

Although she was a good foot shorter than me and slightly built, her grip was like a steel vice, her host imbuing her with far more strength than her looks would suggest. It seemed like breaking her nose had pissed her off quite a bit, as she wasted no time in striking back, swinging her other arm around to catch me across the throat. I just about managed to get my forearm in the way, which saved me from getting my windpipe crushed but nearly took my arm off. Her blow was ferocious enough to push my arm back into my face – hard, and it was only her grip on my other arm that kept me on my feet.

Her older companion had reached me now too, his mouth twisted in a viciously gleeful grin. With only one free arm, which was still numb and heavy, I didn't particularly fancy my chances.

Expecting to regret my choice, but not quite as much as I would getting my face ripped off, I gathered whatever remaining energy I had for one more burst of Magick.

My timing had to be just right, or extremely lucky. Seeing as I was exhausted, in pain, and my vision was starting to go hazy, I'll have to put what happened next down to luck.

As the bearded guy threw his fist towards me, with enough malice behind it to knock my head clean off my shoulders, I channelled all the Magick I had been conserving into my free arm and brushed his fist to one side. It was still pretty touch and go, his hand passing within millimetres of my face.

His expression changed from one of gloating victory to fury, while at the same time I heard the unpleasant cracking and squelching noise over my shoulder, and the grip on my arm went suddenly limp.

While it was tempting to look back and see what had happened, my priority had to be the old guy in front of me. I only had a few seconds left before I ran out of energy, so, taking advantage of his momentary confusion, and the fact that his arm seemed to be stuck, I grabbed hold of his head with both hands and twisted.

The light in his eyes flickered and dimmed before he dropped forward, limp, like a puppet whose strings had been cut, ending up resting against my chest with one arm still over my shoulder. Making an exhausting final effort, I pushed him away from me and was met with the unpleasant sight of his fist still embedded in the skull of the young woman who had been gripping my arm, the two of them slumping to the ground together.

The desire to join them was almost overwhelming. The run from the hospital, followed by expending more Magick than I'd managed in a long time, had pretty much left me running on empty, but staying here was too much of a risk. For a start, it was going to be hard to explain why there were at least two dead bodies in the courtyard with me. Explaining that they were Daemons who had been sent to kill me was likely to only end one way, and I would prefer to stay out of both prison and the City Asylum.

That being the case, I squared my shoulders, made a half-hearted attempt to brush a few fragments of skull from my jacket, and made my way back towards the office.

CHAPTER 10

So, while I stumble my way back, let's quickly address the elephant in the room, or in this case something a bit more than an elephant. So, let's call it the dragon in the room instead, a big sparkly one that vomits unicorns and pisses rainbows.

The dragon in the room is magic, or to give its correct name, Magick, otherwise the ghost of Alistair Crowley is likely to hunt me down and subject me to an eternity of arcane spelling corrections.

It's real, or at least it is here. Back home it might be nothing more than smoke and mirrors, fast talk, and even faster hands, but in this place it can be something far more, something physical, raw, and nasty. Which is why it deserves the extra 'k' at the end.

There aren't many in the City who have the gift, which I guess makes me one of the lucky ones, but it's not the meal ticket you might imagine. Everything has a price.

It's like one of those stores that offer easy credit. You can either wait and save up for something the slow and steady way, or you can get it now, the whole thing set up to be completely painless. Then you get the first monthly bill and realise you'll be paying for that brief moment of convenience for a long, long time.

It's the same thing with Magick. Like it or not, everything takes the same amount of effort, however you choose to slice it. You could break a boulder down to rubble by hitting it with a sledgehammer for hours, or smash it instantly with Magick, then spend the next two weeks with an ache in your arms that you can't shake.

Bottom line, most of the time it's just not worth it. The costs are always greater in the end, the amount of interest the universe charges too high. It's why Arthur got to be King, not Merlin. Merlin might have been able to cast fancy spells, but chances are he spent the next week in bed, trying not to shit out his lungs.

I hadn't even realised that it was something I had in me until a chance encounter opened my eyes.

My mentor in the magical arts was an unlikely Houdini, and one that I had literally tripped over partway down one of the City's less reputable back alleys.

It had also come completely out of the blue. Business had been going well, Samson had stopped being quite so much of a pain in the ass, and I'd got comfortable – too comfortable, a bit cocky even. Not anything like my present-day humble, well-balanced self.

That misplaced confidence meant I had started to take on pretty much any job, regardless of who it involved, and made the mistake of crossing a family who turned out to be better connected and prone to far more violence than I had given them credit for. The twin boys of the family, Frank and Dave, had tracked me down on my way back home one evening, and only their above-average size and below-average intelligence had given me enough warning to change my plans. Overhearing their gleefully muttered threats as they closed in behind me had been enough of a clue to set me off down the nearest alley like an oversized rabbit.

They weren't true twins, or even brothers. No-one has any blood relatives in the City. They did, however, look very similar to each other, having been side by side in the queue when massive foreheads and limited vocabularies were handed out.

It's one of the reasons why the population of the City is

the way it is. Like I said before, you don't tend to get kids who've done enough bad stuff in their lives to get sent here. Second of all no-one here can have children.

The only way the population grows is via the swell of new arrivals, which is balanced by a steady trickle of departures. Most eventually leave via the Elevator in the centre of the City, and the rest through natural attrition. Dying peacefully of old age isn't something that happens here, either.

What it does mean is that there is every nationality, religion, sexuality and political affiliation you could imagine here, good and evil being pretty much universal. It doesn't explain why everyone speaks one language, or why we all end up dressing like extras in a Raymond Chandler novel, but I'm guessing whoever runs this place must be a really big fan of cliché noir fiction.

To be honest, none of that bothers me. I like the style of the place, I'm into jazz and smoky clubs, and I have the kind of head that suits hats, so it's all good as far as I'm concerned.

Anyway, putting the genetics of the place to one side, the bottom line is that two massive Neandertals had made it their mission to pull my arms off. They weren't particularly fast, but they were persistent and lacked the imagination to get bored, which meant they were going to be on my case until I could find a way to lose them.

I was so busy trying to plan a route through the back alleys that I failed to see the hunched, ragged form slouched against the wall. Thinking back, it might not have been quite the coincidence it seemed at the time, but whatever the reason, I managed to trip on the way past, tumbling with a complete lack of grace, my foot tangled in a trailing scrap of material.

"Careful," the pile of rags muttered at me, "you need to pay more attention to where you're going."

I didn't answer, unless you count groaning in pain and

clutching my knee. I had managed to fall awkwardly enough to twist my leg, which now meant I had zero chance of outrunning the two mountains of vengeful dumbness that were lumbering after me. The whole thing was enough to put me in an even worse mood than normal, so being lectured by someone wearing a tramp's hand-me-downs was particularly hard to swallow.

"Fuck off," was my carefully considered response. I tried to get back to my feet, managed to put some weight on my right leg and immediately crumpled back into a pain riddled heap.

"Seems like you're in a bit of a spot," the pile of rags informed me smugly. "Shame you didn't show better manners, otherwise I might have helped you."

Rags had a point, so I tried again. "Fine. Fuck off... please?"

That didn't seem to register either.

"No offence," I added, which is the traditional opening for something particularly offensive, "but how the hell could you help me? Two big, nasty, dumb bastards are heading this way, planning on doing all sorts of interesting things to my insides, and if you get in the way you'll get the same treatment. So, I suggest you take your advice and shove it up your ass, but somewhere away from here."

"Very self-sacrificing of you," my new friend grunted. "Extremely uncivil, but your heart's in the right place."

"At the moment," I replied with half-hearted bravado. "But seriously, you need to clear off now, otherwise you're going to end up dead."

The pile shuddered and slowly rose to reveal the hunched shape of an elderly man, the layers of rags slowly settling behind him into what was possibly the world's ugliest and most rancid cloak.

"Watch and learn," he told me sternly. "After which you and I are going to have a chat about showing respect for your

67

elders. And about moderating your language."

There wasn't much I could do, other than watch. My leg was a complete write-off, so I didn't have a lot of choice. The best I could do was drag myself a couple of metres till I reached the nearest wall. It hurt like hell, but at least it meant I could lean against something and get a decent view of the crazy old man being butchered.

Moments later, the twins arrived, dwarfing my unlikely protector. Underneath the ragged cloak there was almost nothing to him. He looked like a stick insect that had been on a crash diet, but despite that, and the fact that either one of the twins could have picked him up and snapped him with one hand, he looked more chilled out than a snowman on Prozac.

I'd seen all kinds of crazy in the City, and I wasn't getting a whiff of it from the old man. There was something else for sure, something strange beneath the stench of the streets, but madness wasn't part of it.

Deciding that things might be more interesting than I had first suspected, I settled back to watch the show. Frank and Dave weren't quite as perceptive and were grinning like a pair of cats, having cornered an asthmatic mouse.

Frank hit one huge hand into his open fist with a gleeful look on his face. I got the feeling he didn't get out much, and this was what passed for a good night out. The old man blocking his way might have been old enough to be his father, or possibly grandfather, but that didn't seem to bother him. If he'd been even slightly brighter, he might have wondered why the elderly tramp he was facing was so completely unafraid, but he wasn't, so instead he took one lumbering step forward and swung his arm in a slow but extremely heavy haymaker, which should have taken the old man's head clean off his shoulders.

Even though I had been watching the whole thing like a hawk, I didn't see how he managed to miss, or how the old man was suddenly standing behind Dave, halfway across the street.

Frank didn't see either, but that's because he was lying flat out on the ground, a deep purple bruise blossoming on his face and a sizable gap in his smile, where a couple of teeth had been happily residing just moments before.

There was just enough time for Dave's expression to shift from smugly expectant to confused before the old guy touched the side of his head. From a distance, it appeared to be the gentlest of brushes, but from the way Dave tumbled across the street like a ragdoll and the sudden dent in the side of his head, you'd think he'd been kicked by a horse.

By this point I wished that I had been a bit more polite to the old guy, but seeing as how my leg was still busted, I didn't have much choice, other than to hope he wasn't the type to bear a grudge.

He wasn't in any hurry, stopping to prod Frank in the ribs with one grubby foot, before finally making his way across to me.

I tried to stand, failing every bit as miserably as the last time. So instead, he dropped down into an uncomfortable-looking crouch, bringing his face level with mine. Most of his features were obscured behind a huge, bushy beard streaked with grey, but his eyes glinted with the keenest intelligence I had ever seen.

He also had different colour pupils in each eye, one brown and the other almost pure yellow, which was certainly striking, although not very human-looking.

"You killed them?" I asked.

"No. I don't kill. I never kill, not anymore," he replied sternly, seeming to be insulted that I should suggest such a thing.

"It's just…" I paused and pointed across at the two crumpled bodies.

"Bah, they're big strong lads. They'll live," he said. "Might wish they hadn't, come the morning. They'll both have a head-ache they won't forget, and that one," he pointed at Frank, "will be living on soft food for a while."

"So…" I paused again, struggling to choose between the two big universal questions in life, 'why' and 'how'.

Fortunately for me, the old tramp decided to spill the beans on both.

"I bet you're wondering why I helped you out," he said, with a smile that was neither reassuring nor hygienic. Whatever surprising skills he had up his sleeves, the ability to effectively use a toothbrush didn't look like it was one of them.

I shrugged, feigning nonchalance and trying my best to look like a guy who witnessed mad old men beating the crap out of people all the time.

I don't think he was that convinced.

"I could sense potential in you straight away," he told me, still crouched rather too close to my face, adding the unpleasant waft of stale breath to the overall unwashed miasma now drift-ing around us both.

"I thought to myself," he continued cheerfully, "there's a young man who doesn't know what he's carrying around, maybe old Merle can help him out, show him a thing or two about the Magick."

"Magic?"

The old man drew in a breath, mortified. "No, abso-lutely not," he spluttered. "Magic is stage trickery, quick hands and fancy waistcoats. Doves and rabbits and sawing ladies into pieces. What I'm talking about is Magickkkk." He stretched out the final 'k' to make the difference completely clear.

"It's the real thing, the hidden old bones beneath the flesh of the world."

I still wasn't sure how he'd been able to hear the difference in spelling, but the old guy was turning out to be full of surprises.

Calming down, he returned to the matter at hand.

"Everyone has a bit of it running through them," he told me, leaning back in, once again closer than I was comfortable with. "But most people only have a trickle, just enough to occasionally pull a little bit of luck their way."

"So?"

"Heh, that's the big question, isn't it? As I said, most have a trickle, but occasionally you have someone with more than that, enough to change the world."

"Well, it's been fun," I said, trying to push myself back onto my feet. I didn't mind being saved from a beating by a crazy old tramp, but I wasn't going to sit around while he spouted a load of crap about Magic, or Magick... or whatever.

"Don't you want to learn?" he asked, the final word exhaled with some force, leaving me queasy. If his 'Magick' was half as powerful as his breath, he might well be a god of some kind.

Still, I managed to keep my expression carefully blank.

"Learn what, exactly?"

There was an unpleasantly wet sound as Merle's grin widened, lips pulled back from unhealthy looking gums.

"Watch," he told me, resting the tip of one finger against the ball of his thumb. I did watch, even though it didn't seem very exciting.

Then he released his finger, flicking it against my arm.

A few seconds later I regained consciousness, except now I was a good five metres away from where I remembered being slumped. It also felt like an elephant had just tried to trample me to death, and then called all its mates to have a second go... and they'd all been wearing football boots.

It hurt like hell, but I was sold. Whatever it was the old man had just done to me, I wanted to learn some of it.

And so, my training began.

I would love to say that, over time, Merle and I became friends. That his training was firm but fair and made me challenge myself in ways I hadn't thought possible, eventually leading to me unlock the true secrets of Magick. Then, after he'd had a thorough wash, we hugged it out and he admitted to me that I was like the son he never had, a worthy successor.

I would love to say all of that, but I can't, as it would be the biggest crock of shit you ever heard. Merle was, is, and will continue to be, a cantankerous old sod who took great pleasure in making me suffer every single day of my training, and I was delighted when it was over.

They say misery loves company, and Merle is the living embodiment of that statement. I'm not exactly Mr Chuckles myself, but after a day spent learning the basic stepping-stones of Magick, which generally consisted of Merle calling me a 'useless waste of skin' every five minutes, even Samson was welcome company.

Still, whilst the learning experience may not have been enjoyable, he did teach me some pretty helpful tricks, so I guess I owe him that. Slowly but surely, I learned how to feel the flow of Magick through my body. Some people might tell you it's like oxygen or blood, but that's crap. You can't feel blood flowing through your body, it just happens. You might feel a pulse, but that's not the same thing at all. It's far less glamourous than that, much more like indigestion than anything else. You can feel it building up in your body and you know it's going to get released sooner or later, your job is to try and control the timing and direction of its release.

I found out pretty quickly that, without training, most people just fritter their energy away in tiny increments, far too small to achieve anything or even notice. So, the first thing Merle taught me was to recognise the flow and hold on to it, store it up and save it for when you need it.

What he didn't explain to me, to begin with at least, was how the rest of it worked. Particularly the whole thing about feeling like shit the next day. He left that as a nice surprise for me to discover all on my own.

It was one of the few times I think I ever saw him smile, the day after I had managed to use Magick properly for the first time. I hadn't managed anything particularly fancy, just levitating a half-brick for a few seconds, but I'd gone back to the office feeling justifiably awesome about myself and had levitated a few other things, just to show Samson what a spell-casting bad-ass I had become.

The next morning, I couldn't move my arms, rolled heavily out of bed and had a full-on panic attack on the floor. I hadn't made the mental connection between levitating a few household items the night before and my sudden incapacitation. Besides which, I was far too busy swearing loudly at Samson to think things through.

Merle had arrived just in time to stop Samson from clawing my face off and had then spent the remainder of the afternoon explaining the true cost of using Magick. I don't remember exactly what he said, but what I do recall is that he had a grin on his wrinkled face the whole damn time.

Just for the record, I don't believe that Merle is his real name. I asked him about it once. He just smiled and said it was a name that he had learned to live inside. Every name in this place has some sort of meaning, but the 'lifers' like me, Samson, and quite a few others seem to be picked out for extra special treatment when it comes to our given names. Merle struck me as someone who had been in the City for more than his fair share of time, so he should have a name with meaning. But, whatever it was, he wasn't ready to share back when I first asked him, and he never has since.

So, that's us back up to date with Magick. Luckily for me, it's a thing here, otherwise the Envy Daemons would have ripped me to pieces. Unluckily for me, I'll be paying the price for my exertions for a good few days.

CHAPTER 11

By the time I got back to the office, all I wanted to do was have a shower, a drink, and a long lie down. Not necessarily in that order. Sadly, I didn't have time to manage all three, so I settled for a drink.

Although I hadn't exactly enjoyed my run-in with the Envy Daemons, it had proved one thing. There was more to the mysterious girl who had turned up in my office than a simple case of amnesia. Whatever she was involved in was enough to attract the attention of someone with clout. There aren't many people who can rustle up a pack of Daemons. Either that, or I was just extremely unlucky, and my trip to the hospital had coincided with a work outing for the local Daemonic Sports and Social Club.

Samson was out, which was unusual before nightfall. Normally he led a fairly nocturnal social life, spending his daylight hours equally split between sleeping, eating, and giving me a hard time. I used to wonder if he spent his night's meeting up with any other residents of the City who'd ended up stuck in animal form. Some sort of club where they could swap stories and stop feeling quite so alone for a while.

The alternative was that he was out on some sort of romantic tryst. I hadn't ever asked him about his love life, because I didn't want to hear the answer. He was a man trapped in a cat's body, so unless he could find another person who was in exactly the same position, then he was going to have to make some fairly unique choices.

Although I would never admit it to him directly, Samson

was a good listener, especially when I had something on my mind that I couldn't unravel on my own. As it was, it looked like I was going to have to manage without his help for the time being. There were a couple of competing thoughts in my mind about where I could try next, but neither was immediately appealing. I could either go and ask Mrs Jones, or I could pay a visit to the Elevator.

Don't get me wrong, in some ways it would be good to see Mrs Jones again. When I had first found my way into the City and been drawn in by the lights of her club, she welcomed me like a son, looked after me and taught me some valuable lessons. Lessons that meant I'd been able to survive the worst the City had thrown my way. The downside is that Mrs Jones always has an angle. I don't think she can help herself. She's been in the City for so long she's got smog running through her veins and a moral compass that hasn't seen true north in a very long time. After a while, you get tired of being treated like a commodity, so, as much as I still have a soft spot for her, I've been trying my best to stay away.

The Elevator is a completely different matter, but rather harder to explain.

I tossed a coin.

CHAPTER 12

Right in the middle of the City, there is a particularly tall office building. It's a masterpiece of understated steel and glass, simple, elegant, and sharp as a knife. It looks brand new, but I know for a fact that it's the oldest building in the whole place. There's ancient blood running through those shiny metal veins.

Inside, there's a massive foyer, fairly standard in appearance and empty other than a reception desk under the constant watchful eye of Barbara, the scariest receptionist in all of creation, which makes her very, very scary indeed.

Despite her fearsome reputation, I like her. Behind the horn-rimmed spectacles, severe haircuts, and nasty polyester trouser suits, I'm convinced that there's a kind heart. I haven't ever seen any sign of it, but it's there... somewhere. I'm pretty sure she likes me too. The last couple of times we bumped into each other, she didn't even call security. At least, not straight away.

At the far end of the foyer, there's a bank of elevators, although I have only ever seen one of them in use. Normally, you would expect to see a list of floors, and from the outside of the building you would have assumed the place was at least a hundred stories high, but there was just one symbol for the ground floor and two big arrows, one up, one down.

Now and then you would see someone getting in. If the lift is going up, they are normally smiling and light on their feet, although perhaps a little nervous. When the down arrow is illuminated it's a very different story. You wouldn't think that walking into a simple elevator could generate such an extreme emotional response, but I swear I've seen big, tough-looking guys stumbling unwillingly into that small metal box, fighting every step of the way, with a look of such dread on their faces that the memory kept me awake for nights afterwards.

When my time comes, I hope I can take that final walk with confidence and dignity, but I'll probably be the same as all the rest, screaming inside and fighting every single step of the way.

For the record, I've never seen anyone get out of the lift, not ever. If I did, I wouldn't hang around, I would be too busy running for my life.

Tonight, the lifts were quiet, the vast foyer empty, leaving the whole place to me and Barbara. She had clocked me straight away and was looking suitably delighted to see me.

"What the hell do you want, Patrick?"

She didn't sound angry to see me, which was a good start. It was more like the resigned tone of a mother waiting to hear exactly what her wayward offspring had done wrong this time.

"Evening, Barbara. You're looking lovely as ever. That blue really brings out the disapproval in your eyes."

"I told you last time Pat, unless you've got business with the Elevator you shouldn't be here."

She paused, and added in a vaguely hopeful voice, "You don't have business with the Elevator, do you?"

"Afraid not," I replied, "this is just a regular visit. A few questions I hoped you could help me with."

Barbara leaned back in her chair and tapped a couple of times on one of the keyboards spread across her desk, not even making a token effort to hide her disappointment.

Judging by the fact that I was the only one there, and that the building rarely had more than a couple of visitors a day, I doubted whatever she was doing was all that important, but I let her finish her crossword or whatever before I spoke again.

"I need you to check the book for me."

"I've told you before Pat," she said, eyes narrowing behind the thick lenses of her glasses, "the book is private. It's not for the public, and particularly not for you."

"I know," I said, as disarmingly as a bedraggled, bruised, and bloodied individual could manage. "I don't need to see anything. Just check the list for me and see if someone's name is on it, please?"

"And why would I help you? You're nothing but trouble every single time you come by."

She had a point. In the past, I may have caused a bit of a rumpus in the tower. Hence the previous mention of Barbara calling security to 'escort me from the building', which you can translate into, 'beat the shit out of me in the nearest alleyway.'

But that brings me back to the whole 'kind heart' thing. It's no good having a broad streak of decent through you in this place, because someone will take advantage of it. In this case, that someone was me.

"It's not for me. It's a client, a new one. New to me and new to the City. She's just a young girl who's lost, and the more I look into it, the more I think she was never meant to be here. Something's doesn't smell right about the whole thing. So, I need to know whether she's in the book. That's all, nothing else, no details, no secrets."

I can be convincing when I try. Frankly, when you've got a face that looks like it's been run over by a burning shopping trolley, you need to be good with words.

"Fine," Barbara sighed. I'm sure whatever damsel in distress you've run into this time will be worth all the trouble, but just the name. Are we clear?

"Clear," I replied. "Her name is Eve. And she would have

79

been down as an arrival within the last week."

"No second name?"

I shook my head. "She hasn't been here long enough to pick one up. Just Eve." I didn't mention that my client didn't yet know her name, and my only evidence was a grubby hospital wristband. Barbara could be a bit of a stickler for minor things like facts, or honesty. It's why we get on so phenomenally well.

Barbara reached down under the desk and lifted a heavy book onto the surface. It was more like a ledger than anything else. Long, black, and clearly quite old.

It seemed out of place in the shiny surroundings of the office, something that should have been replaced years ago by some sort of spreadsheet or database, yet at the same time, there was a sense of grim permanence about it that made you realise nothing else could ever take its place.

I couldn't shake the feeling that, even when the shiny newness of the surrounding building had decayed into nothing but rubble, the book would still be there, logging every soul in and out of the City, and that Barbara would still be turning the pages.

I have tried to get a peek at the contents more than once in the past, not least to look up my own entry, but it turns out that kind of thing is frowned upon. More seriously, it makes Barbara angry. This time around, I needed Barbara's help badly enough to avoid getting on her wrong side, so I behaved myself and stood at a respectful distance from the desk.

It only took her a minute to find what she was looking for, although I gathered the news wasn't good from the look on her face as she carefully placed the book back under the desk.

"Sorry Pat," Barbara said, taking off her glasses and rubbing the lenses with a tiny chamois. It made a soft, but incredibly distracting, squeaking noise that I tried to ignore.

"She is on the list, and the list says she's due to go down."

"Then the list is wrong," I replied without thinking, surprising myself with the conviction I felt. I actually sounded like I believed what I was saying, which was a refreshing experience. It was just a shame that no-one except Barbara was here to share it with me.

"The list is never wrong, Mr Judas," she said. The switch from 'Pat' to 'Mr Judas' letting me know that I was straying onto thin ice.

It would have been sensible to slowly back away at that point, careful little steps before the ice gave way completely and the frozen water below dragged me under. Instead, I went for the verbal equivalent of jumping up and down with a couple of blowtorches strapped to my feet.

"This time it is. She shouldn't even be here, let alone be scheduled for a trip in the Elevator. Give me a couple of days and I'll prove it."

Barbara paused her industrious glasses rubbing and looked up at me. Despite our various conversations over the years, I don't think I had ever seen her without her glasses on. Looking into her eyes, I was suddenly glad of that fact. The pupils weren't of any discernible colour, shifting between every conceivable shade of green, blue, brown and red so fast that I couldn't keep track, like swirls of paint being mixed on a palette.

I could feel the atmosphere in the foyer thickening around me, suddenly heavy with menace, like the air before a thunderstorm.

It was tricky, but I managed to swallow my pride. At least sufficiently to prevent Barbara from zapping me with whatever supernatural weirdness she had going on. I think I may have mentioned previously that I've gotten pretty good at sensing danger, and at the moment every single early-warning synapse I had was ringing an alarm bell as loud as they possibly could... before running off and hiding.

"Okay… okay," I said, in as calm a voice as I could manage, while giving the universal, open-handed gesture for 'take it easy and – preferably – don't kill me'.

As quickly as the storm had gathered, it dissipated. There I was, back in a very normal looking office, watching Barbara calmly readjusting her glasses and pushing a loose strand of hair back behind her ear.

"So, how long does she have, before…" I asked, nodding in the direction of the Elevator.

"Three days, Patrick. At midnight, as it happens. Like I said, sorry I can't give you better news."

"Thanks for your help," I managed, although my mind was spinning. "I'll see you around."

"No doubt about that," Barbara replied. "No doubt at all."

The walk back to the office passed in a blur. The visit to the Elevator had resulted in far more questions than answers, and tricky ones at that. Barbara going all supernatural on me was the least of my concerns. No-one running the front desk of the Elevator in the centre of Purgatory was going to be one hundred per cent normal, and I had always harboured a sneaking suspicion that there was more to Barbara than met the eye. It had just turned out that there was – a lot more.

A more immediate concern was the news that Eve had a journey booked on the Elevator and that there were only three days until that trip was going to take place. The whole thing made no sense, or if it did, then no-one had shared the news with me.

Why would someone who had only just arrived in the City be destined to leave again within such a short time, and – worse than that – with a one-way trip downwards? Most people didn't hear the call of the Elevator for years, and only when they had achieved enough good, or occasionally bad, in their life to tip the scales of Karma one way or another. Unless Eve had spent all her free time since she arrived on some sort of crazed murder spree, I couldn't see how she'd already managed to qualify for a ticket out of here.

There was something more to Eve's case than I could fathom, and the gnawing sensation in my stomach was telling me it was something big.

I wasn't happy. Every time I get that feeling it leads to a series of nothing but bad things, stacked up one behind the other like big, nasty dominos. I got the feeling that going to the hospital had pushed that first domino hard enough to knock it down, and it was only a matter of time before the rest followed suit, one after another. Problem was, more often than not those dominos were placed in a giant circle, the very last one looming just behind me like a polka-dotted tombstone ready to come crashing down.

Someone had sent the Envy Daemons to stop me, and that meant they had been on to me before I had made my reluctant way to the hospital. Whoever was keeping an eye on me was very well informed, seeing as I tend to keep my business private. I wouldn't get any work otherwise.

By the time I got back to the office, Samson was back in his normal spot, curled up in his basket and snoring quietly to himself. It was tempting to give him a prod, but for once I decided to give him a break. I had too many thoughts bouncing around inside my head, competing for space. There would be plenty of time to get his advice, but it could wait until I had a bit more of a feel for what we were dealing with.

I sank into my chair with a sigh. The morning's exertions had taken their toll, and I knew I was only going to feel worse as the day went on. I had used far too much energy, both physical and magickal, and, although it had kept me alive, before the week was over I was going to wish it hadn't.

My eyelids were just beginning to droop when they settled on a hastily scrawled note pinned to the wall. I recognised the writing as Samson's, which meant that it was barely legible, but still impressive for someone without opposable thumbs. The general gist of it was that Trent had called. I couldn't make out much of the rest, but it looked like the word 'urgent' was in there somewhere.

Although I was exhausted, it seemed that rest and recuperation would have to wait a little longer. I wouldn't generally put myself out, but Trent was a friend. Plus, he was the one who had sent me out on my merry journey to the hospital to begin with, so I supposed it wouldn't do any harm to catch up with him.

I thought I might leave out the bit about the Envy Daemons, or at least the fact I had killed them all. Trent was a good guy, but he did tend to get hung up about things like that. On the other hand, maybe he would feel guilty enough about his advice putting me in harm's way that he would break out a bottle of the really good whisky – the one he kept for special occasions that kept giving me 'I know you want to drink me' vibes every time I looked in its direction.

The evening was drawing in by the time I reached the church, the streets empty, other than the occasional distant and lonely figure wandering through the thinly lit fog. This time of the day, the Church was pretty much guaranteed to be equally quiet. Even the keenest and most lovelorn of Trent's Curates wouldn't choose to walk home after dark in this neighbourhood.

The Church itself was dark, but there was still a warm light illuminating the window of Trent's small makeshift office. Although my muscles were aching and my brain was beginning to sink into a fog made up of too much action and not enough sleep, I was still looking forward to another chance to talk things through with him. The fact that he saw the world completely differently to me often meant that he could send my thought process racing off down an avenue I wouldn't otherwise consider. It didn't always work out, but it's good to walk the world in someone else's brain every once in a while.

I was about ten metres from the closed door to his office when I caught the scent of something cutting through the air. It was a sharp, metallic smell that I knew only too well, one that sent a blast of ice water through my veins. I was running by the time I reached the low doorway and barrelled straight through without stopping, hitting the heavy wooden door with my shoulder like they do in all the movies.

I've done this a few times now and have learned my craft the hard way. What they don't show in the films is what really happens when some poor shmuck tries facing down a couple of inches of solid oak with nothing but some fat, gristle, and bone. The first time I tried barging through a door, I ended up in traction for a couple of weeks, and even now my shoulder can tell rain is coming a few hours before the rest of me.

So, this time I made sure that I had summoned as much kinetic energy as I could manage, forming a buffer down one side of my body that absorbed most of the impact. It was the psychic equivalent of a sumo suit, with a lot of the same drawbacks. As soon as I had myself wrapped in it, my ability to move was vastly restricted, leaving me as graceful as an elephant on roller-skates, but I was already lined up with the doorway, so all I had to do was fall forwards... at speed.

I knew I would have to pay the price for all this magickal showboating the following morning, especially after my exertions earlier in the day, but for the moment, I didn't care. There was a creeping horror waiting for me in Father Trent's office that I couldn't pull away from, even though I desperately wanted to.

You know the feeling. It's the one where you can sense that something awful is behind you and you really, really don't want to look around. In fact, your whole body pretty much refuses to let you. It's like all the bones in your neck have fused into one solid block, but eventually you can't help yourself, pivoting on the spot with your breath held tight and painful, burning deep in your chest.

Remember I said that I struggle with my inner voice, especially during times of stress? Well, this was one of those times.

During those moments, everything slows down, giving me the chance to take in every detail. Shards of shattered wood flying past my face and the inevitable approach of the equally solid and presumably painful stone floor.

I bounced once, rolled awkwardly, and made it back onto my feet, the last of my psychic shield sloughed away like discarded snakeskin. Even with all the Magick I had thrown at it, my arm was throbbing and heavy, but I didn't pay it any attention. Everything I had was focused on the bloody mess sprawled across the small, low desk. It had probably been Father Trent at some point, but I couldn't relate the two. Father Trent had been a compact, genial man, with an expansive forehead, a positive attitude, and a habit of over-pronouncing his vowels. What was left spread across his chair and desk reflected none of that. It was just the left-over flesh that had once contained my friend.

I have seen my share of horrible shit since I've been in the City. Seeing as I've been here a long time, and mainly make my living working for scumbags, that adds up to a whole mountain of the stuff. Still, most of the time I keep it at arm's length, or at least far enough away not to drown.

I don't have much in the way of friends, definitely no family, and I'm not pretty, patient, or pleasant enough to maintain a functioning romantic relationship, so there isn't much that touches me personally. Most of the time it's not much different from watching TV, insulated from the misery of the characters I watch in real life, but this was different.

Father Trent was... had been... my friend. More than that, he had been a good man. Not because he cared about how people saw him, and not because it made him feel better about himself, just because that's what he was.

Someone had taken him from the world, and whoever that son of a bitch was, they were going to pay in blood.

CHAPTER 13

By the time I tore myself away from Trent's place, it was long after midnight. It had felt wrong to leave without saying good-bye in some way, but there was nothing left in that room that I recognised. I tried to get my head down for some rest, but I couldn't sleep. Too many thoughts squeezed into not enough space, all pressed together so tightly that they had started to overlap in my head, creating nasty mental chimaeras that I couldn't shift.

There was Father Trent, his patient smile growing ever wider until it split his head in two. Then Eve searching for her way back home, day after day, week after week. On and on until she grew too old and feeble to look any longer, becoming noth-ing more than another random crazy, shuffling the streets and muttering about the past.

Giving the night up as a lost cause, I stumbled into the office and sank into my chair.

"Bad night?"

Samson was curled up in his usual spot beside the desk, or at least the spot where he spent his time between stalking the streets and rooftops of the City, and terrorising the locals.

I didn't have the energy to answer, but when I turned to look at him the expression on my face was obvious enough.

"Bloody Hell Pat, you look like shit, and a nasty shit at that."

"Heh… thanks, buddy. I love you too. But yes… bad night, and a bad day before that."

I don't think cats were made to look sincere, it's not in their bone structure. They have two expressions, angry or aloof, but Samson was doing something unusual with his face that made me think he was trying.

"I heard about Trent," he said, his voice unusually quiet. "He was alright. Not my kind of guy, perhaps. A bit too heavy on the whole religion thing, but decent enough."

He paused, perhaps he was waiting for something, but I didn't have anything to offer. I had known him long enough not to be surprised he'd already heard about Trent, well before he should have. Whatever network of odd characters he belonged to always seemed far better informed than either the police or the press. I guess it's easy to keep your ear to the ground when you're less than two feet tall.

Standing up in his basket, he arched his back, the closest he could manage to a full-body yawn, and padded his way over to me, jumping lightly onto the desk.

"So, what have we got to work with?"

I rubbed my forehead, hoping to squeeze out a few coherent thoughts. It didn't achieve much, but I managed a few, fairly obvious starting points.

"Someone knew I was going to the hospital, someone who has enough clout to send a gang of Envy Daemons after me."

Samson hissed. He wasn't a fan, partly because Envy Daemons are horrible bastards, and partly because he had a cat-like hatred for what was basically a pack of human hyenas.

Ignoring his bristling, I continued, gaining a little steam.

"Whoever it was also knew about Trent, or at least I presume they did. He said he wanted to see me?"

Samson gave a short nod.

"I don't know what he wanted," he admitted, "but he

seemed keen to speak to you. He didn't seem nervous… exactly, but there was something on his mind."

"But this started before the hospital, and before Trent. I think it all began with Eve," I continued. "Ever since she walked into the office things have been going wrong. I don't know what her deal is, but there's got to be more to her than just another lost soul with memory problems."

I thought back to my visit with Barbara, and the news about Eve's expected fate.

"I got as far as finding out she's scheduled for a trip in the Elevator," I told Samson, who had ceased his pacing on the desk and started to groom his whiskers instead. To someone who didn't know him, that might have seemed a bit rude, but I knew this was the equivalent of stroking his beard or scratching his head. An unconscious habit that helped his thinking.

"Well, she seemed like a nice girl. Perhaps she was good enough to qualify for an early release?"

I shook my head.

"You don't understand Sam, she's due to go down, not up."

"What?"

If I hadn't been so thoroughly miserable, Samson's reaction would've been priceless. He was so shocked he stopped with his paw halfway to his mouth, and nearly dropped backwards off my desk.

"There's no way, she was a sweet little thing. Besides, she's only been here a couple of days."

Over the years we had spent together, I had learned to trust Samson's gut instincts. Most of the time he took an instant dislike to my clients, and nine times out of ten he was proved right, when they turned out to be late-paying, double-crossing, unreliable dickheads.

Whatever the case was with Eve, Samson felt the same

as me, that there was something wrong going on. The problem was, neither of us knew what.

"For a start, there are only a few people I can think of who would have the kind of influence we're talking about," I said, taking the first cautious steps down a line of conversation that I knew led somewhere bad.

"So, what do you plan on doing?" Samson asked. "You going to see Mrs Jones?"

"Not quite yet, there's someone I wanted to check with first. Someone a bit… cheaper to negotiate with."

***

You'd think half the businesses in the City were dive bars, or at least you would if you were walking down the hot mess of streets that made up the 'Reef'. It was a name that some marketing genius had given a gloriously short-lived nightclub, right in the centre of a run-down area to the west of the business district. The developer had grand dreams, the first steps towards a cultural quarter filled with restaurants, cafes and bars. The club itself had died within weeks, but the name had lived on, helped in part by the huge, tasteless sign that had somehow stayed illuminated for months after the club had closed its doors.

The fancy restaurants and artisan cafés had failed to materialise, but low-grade bars had sprung up like neon mushrooms. They offered a place of refuge for those workers in the business district who put in the hours but failed to reap the rewards. Cheap drink, low standards, and the pleasures of temporary anonymity.

Even in the backstreets of the Reef, there was a pecking order. The 'nicer' bars clustered closer to the centre, with Mrs Jones' Club holding court right in the middle. The further from the centre you travelled, the cheaper and more run-down the surroundings became. Eventually, you're not looking at much more than someone's front room with a few chairs and a trestle table passing as a counter.

Lenny's place wasn't quite that bad. It had shelves for at least half of the spirits, some of the scattered chairs had cushions, and the windows still had all their glass. On the other hand, while the building was halfway decent, the clientele and owner were most definitely not.

It was fair, and maybe even generous, to describe some of the characters who frequented Lenny's bar as scraping the bottom of the barrel of life, but Lenny had succeeded in sinking even lower than that. He was what you would find under the barrel, hanging grimly on to the underside and dreaming about how grand it would be to finally climb inside the barrel itself. It was one of the reasons his bar remained popular with a specific sub-set of the City's community. Everyone likes to feel superior to someone, and no matter how bad things were for you, chances are you would be able to look down on Lenny.

Despite his natural disadvantages, he was one of the most enthusiastic and persistent hustlers anywhere in the City. He might have been riddled with more embarrassing ailments than an all-night clinic, but he still viewed life with an outlook so blindingly optimistic that it made me physically sick.

I've shaken Lenny down for information more times than I can remember, and every time he looks at me like a puppy that doesn't know why you're kicking it. Oddly, I never feel even the slightest twinge of guilt or remorse. It's probably because a puppy wouldn't choose to run a bar that caters for the worst scumbags and lowlifes the City has to offer.

It's the way his face lights up when he sees me, his eyes widening in panic, and the way he mouths the words, "oh, for fuck's sake," that makes me feel like I've reserved a really special place in his heart.

Tonight, luck was not on his side. He was so busy serving one of his regulars, his back turned as he loaded up a tray of shots, that he didn't see me until I was right behind him. To his credit, at least he made a half-hearted attempt at running. He didn't get more than a couple of steps. Maybe me grabbing a handful of his shirt was holding him back. With one quick yank, I pulled him over to the bar, and with a second violent jerk bounced his head off the wooden surface, just to make sure he got the message.

"Come on, Judas," he whined, "you haven't even asked me anything yet."

He had a point. Perhaps I should have at least attempted to ask him a question before I started roughing him up.

"Meh," I shrugged. I was just saving time. We would have got to the roughing-up stage in a minute or two, anyway. This way, we could just jump straight to the good stuff and cut out the bits where Lenny pretended he wasn't going to spill the beans.

"I'm looking for someone, Lenny," I told him companionably, but still holding his head down against the bar, just to make it clear we weren't back to being friends just yet.

It says a lot about the clientele that not one person in the place lifted a finger to help him. Everyone knew Lenny was a rat, which made it all the more surprising that he'd stayed alive for so long, and why I always made sure I put on a particularly good show when I squeezed him for information. At least he could claim he had been forced, with plenty of his regulars able to attest to the fact.

"So, who... ouch, bloody hell... who are you looking for this time?"

"I don't know," I admitted, which got more or less the response I was expecting.

"Then you're a bigger prick than I thought," Lenny said, which was pretty tough talk for a guy with his face stuck to a bar.

By now the place was nearly empty, one regular after another having either sidled, crept, or just plain run out the low doorway, like some sort of reverse scumbag osmosis. Pretty much anyone in Lenny's bar was going to be at least two-thirds up to their neck in some sort of criminal activity, and keen not to draw any unwanted attention their way.

This meant I was able to talk a bit more freely, although I still took the opportunity to bounce Lenny's head off the wood-work one more time for good measure.

"I don't have a name," I told him. "But whoever they are, they have enough sway to get a pack of Envy Daemons on their payroll. Someone has made a pact recently, Lenny, and I know you keep your ear to the ground for that kind of thing."

For a minute, Lenny didn't say anything, making me worry that maybe I had hit him a bit too hard this time. Then I heard him giggle, starting quietly, but quickly turning into a full-blown belly laugh.

"You've got no idea what you're getting into, do you?" he managed in between guffaws. "Then you really are nuts... and completely fucked. No-one goes after the Dandy, not if they know what's good for them."

I didn't let it show, but Lenny's answer had hit me in the guts like a sledgehammer. Of all the names he could have given me, the Dandy was the last one I wanted to hear. You'd be better off going after the Devil himself, but I was committed now.

"I'll take that chance, thanks, Lenny. Tell me where I can find him."

To emphasise just how seriously I was taking this, I took one of the more expensive bottles of whisky off the shelf and smashed it on the bar. It left a trail of broken glass and spilt liquor just to one side of where Lenny's face was currently pressed.

"Don't make me do this to you, Lenny," I said. I was being completely honest. I don't mind pressuring low-level assholes like Lenny, but I tend to draw the line at actual physical torture. Normally, the threat of violence is enough, but Lenny was obviously far more scared of the Dandy than he was of me, and that was going to make things tricky.

"You can do what you want, Judas," Lenny spat, sounding like he'd developed a backbone at a really inconvenient time. "I'm not telling you shit. You know why?"

"Why?" I sighed.

"Because the last guy who tried ratting out the Dandy was found in eighteen different parts of the City... and the last part they found was still alive... for a while."

I've seen all sorts of nasty spread across my personal and professional career, but that did sound like a particularly unpleasant way to make a point. Still, it wouldn't do to let Lenny know I felt any sort of concern for his wellbeing.

"I just need somewhere to start Lenny, a name, a place, whatever."

Silence.

Applying some pressure, I pushed Lenny's face a couple of inches along to wooden surface of the bar, stopping just short of the mess of whisky and glass littering its surface.

"I'd hate to mess up that pretty face, Lenny."

"You're a dick!"

I nodded, although Lenny couldn't see. I was being a dick, but I had learned quickly enough that being a nice guy was a guaranteed way to end up very dead, especially in the circles I sometimes have to frequent. Besides, the image of Father Trent, torn to bits in his small study, was still indelibly etched in my mind. If finding his killer meant crossing a few lines I hadn't previously ventured over, I was willing to do it.

At the end of the day, Lenny would heal, or at least he would if the crappy state of his bar top didn't end up giving him face rabies.

Fortunately for Lenny, and possibly for the last little bits of my soul that weren't tainted beyond redemption, I was rudely interrupted before I was forced to carry out my threat.

When I say interrupted, I mean suddenly lifted off my feet and thrown across the room, hitting the wall hard.

The impact winded me and left my vision hazy. It also felt like at least one of my ribs could be broken. But, even with my eyesight temporarily shot, there was a hulking shape across the room that I recognised. It was currently leaning over Lenny, who was making a series of very unhealthy and increasingly desperate sounds.

I had just about managed to get back onto my feet, and most of the stars skittering across my pupils had cleared, by the time the figure finished whatever it had been doing to Lenny and turned my way.

I take back what I said about it being fortunate for Lenny that I'd been interrupted. At the worst, he would have ended up with a couple of interesting scars. Whatever had just been done to him looked far more permanent.

"Sorry, Lenny," I muttered under my breath. I grabbed an unfinished bottle from the nearest table and hurled it across the bar, turning and diving through the window behind me in one smooth move.

Or at least that's how I'd planned it in my head.

In reality, the bottle bounced harmlessly off a table several metres from my assailant, and while I did get through the window, it turned out to be much more solid than it looked.

I took a moment to take stock, pick myself up, and pull a chunk of window from my arm.

"You look like you're lost, Mr Judas. No other reason you'd be hanging around a place like this."

The voice drifting out from inside the bar was oddly wavering, high and cracked. If you didn't know any better, you'd think it belonged to some adolescent boy, still coming to terms with their hormones.

I did know better, which is why I started running.

"Good choice, Mr Judas... not that it'll help you," the voice warbled, bouncing off the high, narrow walls of the alleyway. Then there was a shrill laugh, one that was at least two-thirds of the way down the road to crazy. If he was laughing, then I was in even deeper shit than I feared. It meant that he'd been let off the leash and he could do whatever he wanted to me.

The creepy outline in the bar just behind me belongs to Cain, the complete asshole I mentioned earlier. Like I said, he's been here just as long as me, maybe longer, and I have no clue why the crazy bastard hasn't been sent down where he belongs, but somehow he has clung on to his place in the City by his bloodied fingernails. Maybe he's really kind to orphaned kittens in his spare time, somehow keeping his karma just this side of neutral, or more likely, he has some very influential sponsors. Either way, he was embedded into the darker side of the City. A legend in his own lifetime, like our very own Jack the Ripper, just meaner and less choosy about who he gets to mess up.

The way names work in this place meant he must have been someone seriously bad in his previous life, to end up with 'Cain'. The fact that my name means I did something even worse is worrying, as I'm pretty sure he eats people, or at least bits of them.

"Screw you, Cain," I yelled back over my shoulder.

We have that kind of relationship, having reached the point where we can communicate completely openly and honestly with each other. I'm sure he heard me, although his only response was another laugh. He doesn't do it for effect, the whole laughing thing. He genuinely takes pleasure in chasing people down. The only thing he enjoys more is slowly taking them apart once he's caught them.

He was incredibly light on his feet for a big guy. There was hardly a sound from behind me, certainly nothing that would suggest I was only a few metres away from a big, messy death. The fact that I couldn't hear him didn't mean anything, and I had been doing this long enough to know that looking behind me wouldn't achieve anything other than slowing me down, so I just kept running.

First, there had been the Envy Daemons, and now Cain. Whoever I had managed to upset had got deep pockets, good connections, and no reservations about who they dealt with. Any other time, that would have been useful knowledge to have, something to dig away at in the evening, trying to piece together with the other snippets I had picked up. But, for the time being, I had more important things to do, like staying ahead of two hundred and fifty pounds of crazy.

It had only been a few hours since I'd busted my way through Father Trent's door and the pain in my side was slowly getting worse. I was pretty much running on empty, and there was no chance I was going to use any more Magick without something pretty terminal happening to my insides.

That left me with two options. Run or fight.

**

I had faced Cain once before in a fair fight, and he had taken me down in seconds.

The first thing I discovered during that fight was that Cain was almost supernaturally fast, his apparent bulk a master-class in misdirection. I had assumed, even if I couldn't out-punch him, that I would be faster and could use his size against him.

I knew that big, tough-looking guys often had weak joints, stressed by all the showy weight they were dragging around. I had taken a shot at the knee of his leading leg, a favour-ite opening when I was facing a larger opponent, and one that often worked.

As soon as I had committed to the attack, my heel snapping out for a quick, low kick, I realised I'd made a mistake. It was too obvious a target. The grin on his face the moment before I struck was full of pleasure, as the trap he'd set slammed shut.

Almost quicker than I could see, he'd shifted his weight onto his back leg, my intended attack passing harmlessly underneath its target, leaving me unbalanced for a moment. Before I could recover, he dropped his weight forward again, his foot stamping down on my shin while a fist the size and weight of a bowling ball smashed into my hip.

I don't know if you have ever been punched in the hip? It's not the number one target for most people, who favour more obvious options like the groin or chin, but it hurts like hell and will probably leave you chucking your guts up all over the street.

To my credit, I kept hold of my lunch, but that hadn't been much consolation as he followed up with another couple of fast punches to my kidneys before grabbing hold of my head with both hands. Normally, I would be covering up, ready for the inevitable knee to the face, but my arms were useless dead weights by that point.

The last thing I'd seen had been his rapidly approaching kneecap, while the sound of his high-pitched laughter rang in my ears.

I'm not sure who had been paying Cain back then, but it must have been a lot, as when I came to, I still had all my limbs and organs intact.

From the gleeful tone of his voice and the occasional trill of laughter drifting through the air behind me, I knew he was under no such restriction this time around. He sounded like he was enjoying himself, and that was bad news for anyone in the vicinity.

I started running faster.

CHAPTER 14

You would have thought that, with all the time I spend running away from things, I'd be pretty good at it by now. Unfortunately, I lack stamina, lung capacity, and speed. Generally, I make up for that with an impressive knowledge of most of the backstreets and short-cuts that fill in the gaps between the main thoroughfares. Problem is that Cain knows them, too. He's pretty much the Yin to my Yang, assuming in this case that Yin means psychopathic cannibal.

I had run into a dead end with Lenny, metaphorically speaking, and I suspected that whatever was left of him after Cain's recent visit was unlikely to be sharing any information with me, or anyone, ever again.

I was too far from the office to try heading back there, and besides, I didn't think that would help me much anyway. It would just mean I could enjoy getting tortured and killed in familiar surroundings.

Off in the distance, rising above the rooftops and signalling to me like a gaudy, over-confident lighthouse, I could see the neon lights of Mrs Jones' Club. The same welcoming sign that had drawn me towards the City when I had first arrived, lost and alone.

These days it wouldn't normally be my first choice – my history with the place is a little too complex – but, whatever else you might say about the place, its owner was about as fond of Cain as I was. So, if I could make it through the doors in one piece then I was likely to stay that way... for a while, at least.

I pushed myself faster, taking a sharp right through a tiny

gap between two blocks that hardly even classed as an alleyway, but had apparently been quite popular as a toilet in the not-too-distant past.

I burst out the far end like a cork from a bottle, nearly knocking down a seemingly respectable couple who had been unfortunate enough to be walking past. I had a vague hope that the alley was so tight that Cain might not be able to squeeze his bulk through it, but the guy was like a cat. Not only was he supernaturally light on his feet, but it seemed he could also fit through pretty much any gap, no matter how small.

There was an obvious change between the unpleasant maze of streets I had just exited and the more salubrious surroundings I was now running through, but there wasn't any time to enjoy the view.

The welcome glow of the giant illuminated sign was getting closer, although the sheer scale of the thing meant it was still hard to judge how far away the comparative safety of the Club's entrance was.

The closer I got to the centre of the Reef, the busier the streets became, but with a slightly higher class of clientele. In most cases, that would have been enough for me to slow down. There were plenty of witnesses all around, and if it was anyone other than Cain on my tail then I would have felt safe, but he would just enjoy having an audience.

I was seriously hurting by this point, a combination of exhaustion, stress, and having used far too much Magick, but I only had a few hundred metres to go, and the screams and shouts behind me were getting closer.

That was enough to spur me on for one final half-arsed sprint, taking me across the open square at the front of the Club, past the queue of clearly confused patrons, and almost, but not quite, past the very serious doorman.

I had slowed down enough so that running into his outstretched arm was merely painful, rather than life-threatening.

"Evening, Mr Judas," he rumbled, which was a promising start. "Mrs Jones expecting you?"

"Not exactly," I admitted, trying to resist the temptation to look back over my shoulder "but I have something she'll want to see – urgently."

He turned to face one of the cameras that kept an ever-watchful eye on proceedings, listened intently to the hiss of his earpiece, in the way that only doormen and bodyguards can manage with any credibility, and then lowered his arm.

"In you go then, Mr Judas. Ezekiel will look after you."

It was even darker inside the club than the streets out-side, but it was a familiar and comforting blackness. I allowed myself a deep outward sigh of relief. Tough as the doorman was, he wouldn't be anywhere near a match for Cain, but the door-man wasn't the only security system the Club employed. Anyone trying to cross the threshold uninvited would very quickly find themselves on the receiving end of all kinds of nasty. Cain was smart enough to know that, so, for the moment, I could relax. At least, I could if it wasn't for the fact that I was about to go and see Mrs Jones.

Mrs Jones was another fixture of the City, as permanent as the Club that she kept wrapped around her like a shawl, and she and I have a complicated relationship.

I don't think I've ever seen her away from the dingy shadows and constant drift of nicotine smoke that filled the cav-ernous rooms where half the action in the City took place.

If you want to escape for a while, this is the place to be, forgetting yourself for a few hours, concentrating on the beam of light cutting through the smog and bathing the tiny central stage in a warm, hazy glow, illuminating the motes of dust and dirt swirling through the air like a swarm of lazily circling fire-flies.

That's what the Club does, it takes something ugly in the city and makes it beautiful for a while. That moment doesn't last long – my record is two and a half minutes between leaving the Club and being jumped by a gang in a nearby alleyway, but for those one hundred and fifty seconds, I was pretty happy.

I worked my way into the main auditorium and found an empty seat with a decent view of the stage while I waited for Ezekiel. Tonight, the main act was a petite woman, short dark hair cut in uneven bangs hanging down over an elfin face. She was belting out a dark, velvety ballad with her eyes squeezed closed, hands clenched, filling the room with far more voice than it looked like she could possibly contain. I guess she had a microphone hidden about her somewhere, although I couldn't spot one.

It was a sign of how good she was that the clientele were completely silent, sipping their drinks, smoking their cigars, transfixed, remembering... whatever it was they still could.

It wouldn't last, it never did, but for a while you could feel the sensation of peace laying heavy across the room, sealing the hates and fears that we were all carrying around deep inside, forgotten for a while. Leaving space for memories of something better... of someone better.

Eventually, the last note rang out, the music ended, and the room woke up, shaking itself loose from a briefly shared dream. Off to my side, an elderly businessman blinked a couple of times, looking at the young woman sat snuggled next to him like she was some sort of stranger. I suspect she was, although very much in a professional capacity. Then the momentary look of confusion passed, he lifted his drink with one hand, reached out to squeeze the leg of his companion with the other, and the spell was broken.

I only had to wait a few minutes before I spotted Ezekiel, the club's head barman, part-time bouncer, and Mrs Jones' strong right hand, weaving his way through the Club towards me.

Tall and whippet-thin, with fine, slightly effeminate features, you could easily jump to the conclusion, very foolishly, that he wasn't such a tough guy. But you didn't keep order in a place like Mrs Jones' club by asking nicely. I had seen Ezekiel lift a punter almost twice his weight clear off the ground with one slender arm, before throwing him across the room. I don't know what he eats, but there is a core of steel, sharp and bloody, running through him that you wouldn't want to have aimed in your direction.

Today he had gone for a deep red eyeliner that picked out the darkness of his eyes and matched the burgundy lining of his suit. Always a snappy dresser, I could see the bemused despair in his expression as he slowly looked me up and down, taking in my tattered jacket.

"Ahhh, Judas, looking… unique, as usual."

"Hi, Ezekiel, how's business?"

"Good, Judas. It's always good."

The perfunctory niceties out of the way, he gestured across to the stairway at the far side of the club. "Mrs Jones says she will see you now."

I nodded, pushing back my chair and getting to my feet.

"She also says remember to behave yourself."

I nodded again, although I didn't need telling. I might not have that many airs and graces, and in my time I have been thrown out of pretty much every club, bar, or dive there is, but I had never caused a problem in Mrs Jones' place. I suspect that she'd said no such thing, but Ezekiel had a reputation to uphold, and if that involved telling me to behave, then so be it.

Over the years, Mrs Jones had increasingly kept herself in the background, and Ezekiel had become her mouthpiece as well as her right hand. When I first arrived, she had been a constant presence, working the room like royalty, shaking hands, kissing cheeks, maintaining influence. Recently, she had left more and more of that side of the business to Ezekiel, spending the majority of her time locked away in her office high above the rest of the club. She had always been a big woman, matronly and warm, enveloping her friends, guests, and business associates within the comfort of her company and favour, but as the years passed, her health had deteriorated and she had increasingly struggled to move as easily as she once had.

Following obediently after Ezekiel, I made my way to the stairway that linked the ground floor of the club with the mezzanine containing Mrs Jones' office and a small suite of rooms that now served as her accommodation.

Stepping to one side and gesturing up the stairs, Ezekiel gave a half nod, allowing me to pass. I could feel his gaze on my back as I made my way up, stopping as I reached the summit. It wasn't very often that I got to see the club from this perspective, perched up above the crowds. On the increasingly rare occasions I had the chance, I always savoured the view.

The first time I stood in this spot, it had been alongside Mrs Jones, intrigued despite myself by the ebb and flow of the patrons below us.

"You can see all the patterns of the City from up here if you have the patience for it," she had told me, amused by my fascination. Although her tone had been playful, gently mocking, there was a serious undercurrent to her words that made me pause and take a proper look.

To begin with, I had struggled to see what she meant, the whole scene seeming to be completely random and chaotic, but she had been in no hurry, and so I'd stood, leaning against the high rail, watching, and waiting.

It was like one of those optical illusions. A mass of lines and colours that initially appears to show nothing more than a meaningless mess. Some people have the knack of seeing straight through them, but for me it was always hard work. The trick is to let your mind relax, to stop trying too hard, letting your gaze settle on an imagined point somewhere behind the picture itself. It always seemed completely impossible, with no sign of the car, or dog, or whatever it was you were supposed to see, then just as I was about the give up, the hidden image would emerge like a ship from a bank of fog.

The eddying tides of lost, drunken humanity down below the mezzanine were the same. At first glance, there was no order, no meaning to the apparently random movements, but the longer I stood there, the more the constants amid the chaos become clear. Nestled snugly in one corner was a table with a steady stream of arrivals and departures, each straight into the club and straight out, pure business, no pleasure stops for drinks or company. Across the floor, a couple of the hosts and hostesses Mrs Jones employed to work the customers sparkled at the centre of ever-changing circles of patrons, each new group sucked in and spat out just as quickly. On the other side of the club, a well-dressed man in a light grey suit strutted around as if he owned the place. I'd briefly clocked him on my way in, dismissing him as some ridiculous pretender, his walking cane an unnecessary and attention-seeking affectation.

Once I paid him a bit more attention, he appeared rather less laughable, and I saw more clearly his slowly expanding influence. For one thing, there were several large shadowy figures that never seemed far from him. Never close enough to be obvious, but always watching, ready and waiting. One after another, patrons of the club would approach him, sometimes on their own, sometimes in couples, but always with signs of obvious wealth and influence. He would favour them with a few words, a handshake, then move on.

I knew then I was on the cusp of working something out, fitting all the pieces together, the ostentatiously dressed man with the walking cane, the circulating hosts, the table in the corner, all part of one interlinked ecosystem. My fledgling investigative senses were scratching at my brain like fingernails on a blackboard. I hadn't realised until later that I had been looking for the first time upon the man who would become known all across the City as 'the Dandy', a whispered name synonymous with organised crime, violence, and fear.

Then Mrs Jones had tapped me on the shoulder, breaking my concentration and dragging my mind back to the business at hand.

I often thought back to that first night, perched up above the Club, like a bird of prey scanning the world below, and wondered why Mrs Jones had encouraged me to try and make sense of it all. What she had been trying to show me?

***

There were still patterns. I had learned to see them more clearly now, not just in the club, but all across the City. I have to say, they were never as clear or as well connected as they had been that first night.

Even tonight, with business in the club slower than usual, I could spot a few ripples in the great pond of life, but nothing major. Just minnows trying to get themselves noticed rather than indications of anything bigger skulking somewhere below the surface.

Tearing myself away from the balcony, I made my way to Mrs Jones' office, shielded with darkened glass that made it impossible to see in, although I knew from experience the view from inside looking out was crystal clear. The door was solid, banded with steel, and lacked any sort of visible handle, keyhole, or window. There was a small thumbprint scanner half-hidden in a recess just to one side and a pair of cameras staring accusingly down at me. Giving a friendly wave to one camera, which I know annoys the hell out of Mrs Jones, I placed my right thumb on the scanner and waited.

Maybe she was busy doing something else, or perhaps it

was because of the wave, but she kept me waiting.

It was tempting to try the scanner again or knock on the door, but I wasn't going to give her the satisfaction. Instead, I got to stand around outside the door like a naughty school kid waiting for the headmistress to let them in to her office.

Finally, there was a click and a hiss, and the door slowly slid to one side. As always, the inside of the office was drenched in darkness. I knew from experience this was pure showmanship, not least because Mrs Jones had told me so.

I had to hand it to her though, it might only be smoke and mirrors, but the whole thing worked. The cameras, the scanner, the hiss of the door, and the darkened interior. Everything conspired to make it clear you were entering somewhere special, and that you'd better mind your manners.

My night vision is pretty good, helped out by the fact that my working hours are often nocturnal, but I still couldn't see more than a metre ahead of me. From memory, Mrs Jones would be sat behind her huge desk, carved from a single lump of Acacia Wood. It had cost a fortune, but, like the cameras and scanner, it was all part of the image that she wanted to imprint on anyone fortunate enough to be granted an audience.

"Evening, Patrick."

Her voice was every bit as warm and voluptuous as the rest of her. She had a habit of lingering over words, dragging each syllable through treacle before letting it loose.

"Mrs Jones," I nodded in greeting, well aware that even though I couldn't see her, you could bet she could see me.

Sure enough, there was a click, and the room was bathed in light. For a moment a ripple of orange and yellow flowed across the dark wood of the desk, drawing my eye to the woman who sat behind it. She was still an impressive sight, whatever the passing of time had inflicted upon her. She was dressed in a deep purple that complimented the smooth, unblemished darkness of her skin, accented with one simple brooch in the shape of a dove in flight.

"Have a seat."

Mrs Jones gestured with one languorous wave of her hand, in the general direction of the leather chair on the near side of the desk. Seeing as it wasn't really a question, I complied and sat myself down, bringing me face to face with the Club's long-time matriarch, and the closest thing I have to a mother in this sorry place. Not a particularly caring or considerate mother, and one that was liable to have me killed if I stepped too far across whatever invisible lines she was working to this week, but a mother, nonetheless.

When I had arrived in the City, lost and alone, with nothing but a nametag and a hospital gown, somehow I had found my way to the door of her club, and, rather than cast me back into the street, Mrs Jones had taken me under her wing. She had seen something, some potential that I had never quite managed to realise. More recently, our meetings have been tainted by her underlying disappointment, which is frustrating as hell, as I don't know what she's disappointed about. It was there even now, lodged just behind those large, torpid eyes.

"So, what can I do for you?"

"Why do you always assume I want something?" I began, but even with Mrs Jones staring me down like a sleepy basilisk, I couldn't keep a completely straight face.

"Fine," I admitted, giving her my most winning smile, which had about as much effect as a dehydrated kitten spitting at a wildfire, "I do want a bit of help, but that doesn't stop me from being happy to see you."

"You too, Patrick... you too." Mrs Jones smiled back. The slow, lazy smile of a shark that, for the moment, has decided to swim in the same direction as you.

Before going any further, she stopped and poured out a

couple of large drinks. She knew me well enough not to ask, pushing mine across the desk with a slight grunt. As always it was bourbon, an expensive one that warmed my guts and made me want to be a better person, or at least a richer one.

"So, what are you after?"

I took one more gulp of my drink, hoping I would still be welcome after the question I was about to ask.

"I need to find the Dandy," I told her, watching for her reaction. It was a complete waste of time, her face giving away nothing. Behind that listless, disinterested expression, I knew the tightly coiled machinery of her mind was whirring, balancing risk and reward, running through every conceivable scenario, and hopefully taking into account whatever narrow sliver of affection she still felt for me.

It was a big ask. The Dandy had become a byword for organised crime in the City, a boogieman you whispered about, hoping you wouldn't attract his attention. But he was still just a man, and one that used to frequent Mrs Jones' club before he'd become a legend. To find him, you needed to be connected, with roots running deep into the underworld. The woman sitting opposite me was about as well connected as you could be, her club the hub around which the dirty wheel of the City revolved.

It didn't mean she was untouchable, though. No-one is. The heavy security wasn't just for show, so giving me a lead on the Dandy wasn't something she would do lightly. It would be nice to think that our long relationship carried some weight, but I'm a realist, and while I'm sure the pleasure of my company was something Mrs Jones valued, she was going to want something extra.

I didn't say anything more to try and sway her. I had something better than words. The downside was that this was a card I could only play once. I reached inside my coat, pulled out a small envelope and pushed it across the desk. I had been toying with the idea for a while, putting off seeing Mrs Jones for as long as possible, but subconsciously I had known I was going to end up at this point sooner or later. I should listen to my subconscious more – it would save a lot of time.

One gloved finger pinned the envelope in place before she picked it up and pulled out the content. It contained a single photograph, one that I'd been holding on to, something for a rainy day. Parting with it was going to be hard, but I didn't have much choice.

Her reaction wasn't quite what I expected. Her eyes lit up, and a yelp of laughter escaped from heavy lips that rarely showed any genuine emotion.

"Oh, Patrick, this is fabulous... oh my! oh my! Looks like Harland has been a very naughty girl in her spare time."

I'm not going to go into the details, I'm too much of a gentleman for that. Let's just say that, a few months ago I had been tailing someone for a client, looking for some dirt they could use as leverage, and ended up with the added bonus of finding Chief Harland in some highly compromising and very niche company. Don't ask me why she'd taken the risk, someone in her position should definitely know better and would generally have several advisors, minders, or lackeys to make doubly sure.

Maybe she was fed up with always being a control freak ice queen, or maybe she just got drunk one night and made a really shitty decision. Whatever it was, it had gifted me one hastily snapped photo that I had been keeping safe ever since.

It was an odd sort of insurance policy, one that could play out in one of two ways. Either it was worth a fortune and would give me a chance to pull on one of the levers of power that ran the City, or it was a death sentence, with Harland and her cronies willing to do whatever it took to cover up her indiscretion.

Of course, there was also a third option, and that was to pass it on to someone else. Someone influential enough to get far more mileage from it than I ever could.

Tonight seemed as good a night as any to trade it in, find out if the power this snatched photo held was enough to buy my way to the Dandy. So I sat and watched and waited... and drank quite a lot more of the bourbon.

Mrs Jones took her time, the same way she did with everything, but she didn't take her eyes off the photo the whole time, which made me think I was on to a winner.

"You got any more of these?" she eventually asked.

"No, just the one."

"You're not worried that I might just take it. After all, even owning this photo is enough to drop you into a world of hurt."

Her tone was light and airy, but the implied threat in her words was clear. I knew that if she wished it, I wouldn't leave her office, or at least not in the same state I'd entered. But, terrible as Mrs Jones could be, I didn't think murdering me without a really good reason was completely her style.

I hoped I was right.

Giving the photo one final look, she drew in a whistling breath, then secreted it away in the nearest draw. I couldn't tell if she was scandalised or impressed, although I suspected the latter.

"I can't tell you where the Dandy is, Judas," she said, "and even if I could, I wouldn't. That man has his tentacles everywhere in the City, and some nasty dogs at his beck and call when he needs them – your old friend Cain amongst them."

I should have slammed my drink down, caused a scene, demanded the photo back, but I didn't. I knew Mrs Jones better than that, so I sat and waited for the rest of the conversation to play out.

"There is something you can do for me, though," she

added, almost as an afterthought. "There's an old factory down in Seventh that has some unsavoury sorts squatting there recently. I could do with someone going and checking that they haven't spread to any of my properties. I like to keep things clean and tidy. I'm sure you understand."

I did, or at least I hoped I did. Nodding my thanks, I took a final gulp of the bourbon and made my way back out.

"Ezekiel will give you the details," she called after me. I looked back over my shoulder just before the door slid closed, but she wasn't looking my way. Instead, she was rocking gently in her chair and chuckling to herself.

I wasn't fully sure what I had unleashed by sharing that picture, but I was sure Mrs Jones would be making the most of it, and soon. The best thing I could do was follow up her not-very-subtle lead and get down to the old industrial district before the whole City started going to hell.

Ezekiel was waiting for me as I reached the bottom of the stairs, handing me a book of matches with a single address written inside the lid. Any other place in the universe you would get a sheet of paper with the address, or an email, or text, but not in the City. There's a certain way that things have to be done here, and secretive addresses written in matchbooks is one of those things. The whole place is cliché as hell... but who I am to talk?

He also handed me a bottle, which, to my great pleasure, was the same bourbon as I'd just been enjoying in the office.

"Compliments of the management," Ezekiel said, without any obvious irony.

Damn, the guy was efficient. For one disloyal moment, I wondered what it might be like to have an assistant who was competent, or helpful, or human, but then the moment passed. Sure, Ezekiel might be good at his job, and a scary bastard when he needed to be, but I bet he couldn't lick his own arse.

The address wasn't one I recognised, but I knew the area

well enough. It was a district of the City that had been the subject of a series of glossy announcements from City Hall a few years ago. Investment in industry, growth and prosperity. Jobs for all, that sort of thing.

None of it ever came to anything. The place was still a run-down shithole, with half the units empty and the rest occupied by short-lived ventures unable to afford anything better. It made sense that the Dandy might be there. The combination of cheap real estate, limited oversight, and a lack of any sort of police presence was pretty much perfect.

Still, it was far too late to go there now. I needed to go back to the office and get my head down for a good few hours and hope that Cain had buggered off for long enough for me to do that without waking up dead.

CHAPTER 15

The journey back to the office was nerve-wracking, but there was no sign of Cain. I assumed he'd gone to hang upside-down in his crypt, or whatever it was he did at night. That reassuring thought was completely ruined by the sight that greeted me as I walked up the last couple of stairs leading to the landing and the doorway to my tiny domain.

The door was hanging off its hinges, with most of the glass from the inset panel spread across the floor. A few crunching steps took me across the threshold, allowing me a proper look at the carnage inside.

The office had seen better days. In fact, it had never seen a worse one. Never tidy at the best of times, my filing system had become increasingly reliant upon remembering which of the teetering piles of papers balanced about the place contained my latest case files, which contained urgent bills, and which were safe to leave untouched for another month or two. I'm pretty sure that the papers at the bottom of a couple of the piles were starting to fossilise.

Whoever had busted in the door had done a similarly thorough job on the rest of the place, and my once comfortably familiar stacks of paperwork were scattered haphazardly across the office.

Every drawer of my desk had been pulled open, a couple completely removed and left upended on the floor, little wooden rafts abandoned on the chaotic sea of paperwork covering most of the floor.

Even Samson's basket had been turned over, the old cushion moulded over the years into his exact size and shape ripped into pieces, its cheap stuffing mixed in with the rest of the surrounding mess.

A shiver ran down my spine... Samson. He'd been here when I left and wasn't one for going out during the day, preferring to preserve his energy for his night-time liaisons. If he had been here when the office had been hit...

Whoever did this had been in a hurry, not worried about making a noise or a mess, and that would presumably include taking apart anyone unfortunate enough to be in the place.

Samson could be a miserly pain in the ass, but I had gotten used to him being about the place, so the thought of some thug carving him up wasn't something I wanted to settle in my brain for too long. On the plus side, I couldn't see any chunks of fur or splatters of blood, which could be taken as a good sign. On the other hand, the fact that he could talk meant he could be questioned, so perhaps whoever had done such a good job of tearing my office apart had also dragged Samson away to somewhere where they could wring some answers out of him in their own sweet time.

I'm not a huge fan of being tortured, although in my long and colourful career there have been a couple of occasions when I've had the misfortune. It certainly wasn't something I wanted Samson to go through. Firstly, because it was an awful, stomach-churning, mind-flaying experience that no-one should have to experience, and secondly, I was pretty sure he would give me and all my secrets up in a matter of minutes... and then they would kill him. I wasn't sure how many of his nine lives he had left, but it was unlikely to be enough.

Even with the shock of what I had stumbled into, my mind was whirring away, spotting potential clues, cross-checking them against any facts I was already sure of. My paper filing might be a complete disaster, but part of the reason everything still works is because I am unusually good at mentally collating and storing information. It's handy in my line of work, filling my head with a huge archive of information that sometimes bubbles up to the surface at the perfect moment, although it just as often leaves my brain clogged up with facts and figures I no longer need.

I'm guessing that all the space that would normally be filled with regular things like memories goes spare when you end up in the City, and I'd found a way to put that unused storage to good use.

The damage to Samson's bedding was one example. What I had initially taken for cuts in the material was, on closer inspection, a series of rough tears, uneven and ragged. Another was the door to the office, which had been kicked in from the outside. It had taken a good deal of force, with the main impact just below the glazed panel, where the wood had splintered, giving me an idea of the possible height of the intruder. My first thought was that it had been Cain. The violence of the damage, the strength of the intruder – they all added up, but I wasn't sure.

Although whoever had done this had been in a hurry, the office had still been turned over pretty thoroughly. They had presumably been looking for something very specific, but the carnage spread haphazardly across the floor meant it would be a good long time before I realised what, if anything, was missing.

Picking up one of the chairs from where it had been toppled over, I sat down and took a minute to survey the rest of the room. It allowed me to calm down and disturb as little as possible until I had taken everything in, avoiding the immediate temptation to go tramping around the room and inadvertently obscure any remaining snippets of information that might lead me to whoever had done this.

I've crossed paths with plenty of people who were more than capable of this sort of thing, but the disregard for subtlety and the speed with which the search had been carried out suggested urgency.

There was only one recent job that seemed likely to have got under someone's skin enough to lead to this sort of reaction, and that was the one Eve had brought to my door.

"Bloody Hell, Pat! What on earth have you done to the place?"

My musings were disturbed by the sound of a very familiar and welcome voice.

Samson was stood in the wreckage of the doorway, a look of almost comical confusion on his face.

"I thought I'd spring clean," I managed, which wasn't the pithiest comeback ever, but I was having a really bad day, and there was no way I could let him know I was happy to see him.

"Yeah, my sides are splitting, Judas. Seriously, man, look at my bed!"

"I think I might have pissed off some important people," I admitted, which received pretty much the expected reaction.

"No shit. I told you going to the Elevator and poking your nose around wouldn't end well." His fur was bristling, although I don't think he was particularly angry at me, he just didn't like people messing with his stuff. It's a cat thing.

"Any idea what they were after?" he added, lifting a paw to fastidiously step over a damp patch where a bottle of whisky lay smashed. Whatever else the intruder had achieved, my floorboards were now 40% proof and more flammable than a heavily insured firework factory.

"Not a clue. Mrs Jones gave me a lead on the Dandy, but I'm not even sure he's behind all this. All I'm working from is the word of Lenny, and he's not famously trustworthy," I said. "Although the fact that he got offed by Cain just afterwards has to count for something."

Samson sighed and shook his head. "Story of your life, Pat. Just smart enough to work stuff out, just dumb enough not to realise what."

"Yup," I admitted, slumping down further into my seat, which was starting to feel amazingly comfortable, despite the wreckage around me. "Tell you what, I'll just have a little sleep, then we can work out what to do next."

"You do that, Pat," Samson replied, resisting the temptation to say anything more cutting. I think he could tell I was having a hard time. In the last twenty-four hours, I had been beaten up twice, seen the insides of one of my best friends spread across the floor, given away the only leverage I had, and ended up likely to have Cain breathing down my neck for the foreseeable future. It had been a pretty shitty day.

Tomorrow would be better. Unless, that is, I did something extremely dumb – like going looking for the Dandy, in which case it would probably be a lot, lot worse.

CHAPTER 16

Waking up wasn't nice. I had been dreaming, although, as always, the memory slipped through my fingers before I could see the shape of it. Everything hurt, the trials and expenditures of the previous day coming back to claim repayment with a vengeance.

My mouth tasted like the interior of a septic tank, and my head felt like a battalion of termites were trying to dig themselves a new home. The rest of me wasn't much better. Sleeping in a chair hadn't helped, but I was already so beaten up that a bad back wasn't going to make much difference.

I wasn't sure what time it was, but there was some natural light spilling in through the window.

Even more unusual than the sight of some sunlight, insipid as it might be, was the sight of the office, which was… fairly tidy. It was still completely ruined, but the mess had been put into piles and most of the broken glass was gone. There was even a new door hanging in an equally new looking frame.

"What the hell?" I muttered.

"Ta-dah," Samson swanned into view, looking extremely pleased with himself. Seeing as cats are naturally pretty smug-looking anyway, you can imagine how unbearable he looked.

"Pretty good, eh, Pat?"

I just nodded dumbly. I knew he was a little more capable than your average feline, but fixing doors seemed likely to be beyond even his talents.

His cocky demeanour wound down a notch momentarily

as he continued.

"I did call in a couple of favours, but it struck me that we needed to improve our security, and a working door seemed like one of the basics."

"Favours from who?"

Samson changed gear again, from unbearably smug to unmistakably shifty.

"Oh, you know, friends, colleagues... favour givers."

By now, all sorts of alarm bells were ringing. Samson knew, as well as I did, that we were pretty short of friends, and entirely out of colleagues. There were only a couple of options I could think of, and neither of them were welcome.

I took another look at the new door. In contrast to the last one, the replacement was solid wood, top to bottom, with no glass panel. Now I was waking up a bit I was able to spot a few other details that set it aside from its predecessor. Not least was the fact that the inside looked like it was covered in a mass of random-looking markings. To the untrained eye, you might think that an angry child had been set loose on it with a pack of giant crayons, but I had learned enough to recognise the scribbling as something far more intentional.

"Bloody Merle," I muttered to myself, although it was loud enough for Samson to overhear me, as he took a slight, sheepish step backwards. "I told you he's not welcome around here, and I don't want his help. The man's an untrustworthy shit."

"I know," Samson replied. "I didn't call him, I swear. But you have to admit that he's done a good job on the door. Covered it in so many hexes, hoodoos, and whatnots that even Cain would struggle to get past it."

It pained me, but Samson had a point. With a batshit crazy psychopath like Cain on my case, having a bit of added security about the place, magickal or otherwise, seemed pretty sensible. Then the rest of what he had said sank in.

"Wait a minute. If you didn't call Merle, who did?"

If anything, Samson looked even more nervous, which was unusual, as he doesn't normally care what I think about anything. I couldn't think of anyone who would be more of a problem than Merle, other than...

"Gaby," he admitted. He didn't give me the chance to say anything before he carried on, obviously deciding to make a clean breast of it, although it didn't alter the defensive tone in his voice.

"Well, what did you expect me to do, Pat? The office was wrecked, you were a state, and there was every chance a raging psychopath was going to bust into the place and kill you in your sleep... and me while they were at it. I'm not quite ready for that yet, thanks."

I didn't say anything. I knew he was right. Any normal person would be grateful, but I couldn't think of anything to say. Hearing her name was still enough to knock me off my feet, and that fact that she had been here, looking out for me, even after everything that had happened, was too difficult to absorb. Perhaps after some proper sleep, or a drink, or a couple of days in a row when I wasn't bleeding everywhere, then things would make more sense.

After a couple of minutes of increasingly awkward silence, I found my tongue. I didn't have much choice. There's no way anyone could outstare a cat, even a sorry excuse like Samson.

"So, how was she?"

"She was doing fine, Pat," he told me with a knowing glint in his eye. "Looking good and doing pretty well for herself, too. She's worked her way up in the world, which was lucky for us. She had enough sway to get Merle over here in double time. You should catch up with her, straighten things out. It would be good for you."

"Yeah, I'll make sure I do that… soon."

It was pretty obvious my fingers were crossed. Perhaps I should have put my hand behind my back first. Still, it was a step in the right direction. A little, tiny baby step.

Samson was still grinning at me. I uncrossed my fingers and waved them in his direction.

"But it'll have to wait. Mrs Jones gave me an address for the Dandy, and I doubt the trail will stay warm for long. The guy's a ghost."

"Sure, Pat. I'll be waiting with the band-aids when you get back," Samson replied with a sigh.

I didn't bother getting changed, just had a quick stand-up wash, enough to clear most of the previous day's grime and stop my mouth from tasting like a dumpster fire. Then I was off, although only after reminding Samson to lock our new extra-special door behind me.

CHAPTER 17

The area where I'd been told I could find the Dandy was an underwhelming maze of old units which were either derelict, housing businesses that were shady enough to want to stay out of the limelight, or so unsuccessful that the occupants were unable to afford anywhere better.

Unusually for me, I managed the entire journey without any sort of mishap, ambush or other distraction, and there was even a touch of sun still visible through the smog. It wasn't the kind of build-up I had expected. The Dandy had been a monster under the bed, whispered about but never acknowledged, and something of an obsession of mine ever since I had first spotted him all those years ago in Mrs Jones' club. There should have been heavy clouds hanging over the city and lightning arcing through the sky, a flock of crows circling overhead, and maybe even some random crazy with an 'end of the world is nigh' sign to see me on my way.

But there had been none of that, just a spot of sunshine and a brief encounter with a nice old fella selling hotdogs, which had added a few entirely pleasant minutes to my journey.

Still, I wasn't naïve enough to think any of that meant anything. Somewhere in the sprawl of warehouses around me was the Dandy, and he was going to pay for what had been done to Trent. Once blood and revenge are brought into the mix, nothing else matters. It just made me savour the relative peace and normality of the morning even more, painfully aware it wasn't going to last.

I stopped for a minute to check the details Ezekiel had

given me. The building I wanted was nearby, set back slightly from the road, hidden away behind the sad, decaying carcass of an old distribution yard. The tarmac had long given up its uneven fight with nature, and now the surface was rippled with the ingress of weeds and the first green shoots of low bushes and saplings. There's probably some sort of moral lesson about the inevitability of life or the temporary nature of humanity behind it all, but I didn't care. It just meant I had to watch my step as I crossed the yard, trying my best to appear like a nonchalant passer-by who just happened to be going for a stroll through an abandoned industrial site, miles from anywhere.

I wasn't fooling anyone, but on the other hand, there didn't seem to be anyone around to fool. I had been expecting some pretty heavy security around the Dandy. Nothing too obvious, but there all the same. By now, I should have triggered enough interest for there to be at least one laser sight lighting up my forehead, but I wasn't feeling anything. There was a small building opposite the Dandy's warehouse which would have made a perfect nest for a sniper to cover the approach, or at least that's where I would have picked.

I don't know what motivated my change of heart, other than an increasingly uncomfortable tingle that something was seriously off, but I decided to take a slight detour and check out the smaller building first. It looked like it had been intended as a little starter unit, with a small industrial space on the ground floor and an office above. The door wasn't locked, and pushed inwards easily and quietly, which made me think it had been oiled recently, despite the derelict state of the surroundings.

The ground floor was completely barren, lacking even the bare bones of whatever short-lived business had temporarily called it home, so I tried the stairs to the first floor. This had been set up as a mezzanine, only covering half the footprint of the building, but with a pair of large windows that looked directly across at the Dandy's warehouse. As with the ground floor, the original contents of the place had been stripped. Either cleared out when the previous occupant's business folded, or picked clean shortly after. But it was clear that, more recently, the place had been used by someone new, with a deckchair set up close to the window, a small table with a radio, and a pile of books. To my complete lack of surprise, there was also a high calibre rifle leaning against the wall between the two windows.

What was a lot more surprising was that the deckchair was still occupied, by a middle-aged man with a high forehead, short-cropped dark hair, just beginning to turn grey, and a big messy hole where his chest would normally be.

It explained why I hadn't been challenged up until now, but it also meant that I wasn't the only one here for the Dandy, and judging from the still quite sticky looking remains in the deck chair, my competition had been here very recently.

The thought that anyone who fancied going up against the Dandy was either insane or extremely dangerous was one that I shoved to the back of my mind. So, instead of agonising over things, I ran back down the stairs, straight across the road, and up to the warehouse. It wasn't far, but I was still on the down curve from all my exertions of the previous couple of days. By the time I reached the relative shelter of the entrance, I was breathing hard.

The main entrance was sealed tight, metal shutters pulled down and, by the look of them, welded closed. A quick circuit of the building was all it took to find an entrance, one that looked like it had already been used.

Around the back, one of the roller shutters was opened halfway. That was the first clue. The second was the remains of two very recently and messily deceased men. Both were big and tough-looking, although not tough enough, as one was missing his head and the other had a hole in his chest just like the guy across the courtyard.

Apparently, whoever else was here had taken this route too, stopping just long enough to make a mess of the guards. Either that, or the Dandy had really let his health and safety standards slide.

Ducking under the shutter and trying not to get too much blood on my shoes on the way, I entered the Dandy's lair.

The inside of the warehouse was huge, bleak, and empty. There was a thick layer of dust across the majority of the floor, suggesting that most of the building had been out of any active use for quite a while, although there were also several trails where recent footprints had disturbed the settled grime.

In one corner there was a doorway to a smaller area of office space, which is where all the more recent footprints seemed to be headed.

The door to the office was far more substantial than you would expect, at least two inches thick, reinforced with metal sheeting and a complicated locking system that seemed to involve a retina scan, some sort of fingerprint recognition, and a keypad.

None of this bothered me, as the door was wide open. What did concern me was the fact that whoever had last used the locks had left a few things behind, including the severed end of a finger and an eyeball. I'm not one to jump to conclusions, but when someone or something starts leaving body parts lying about the place like a set of discarded keys, my first instinct is that they might not be all that nice.

Reaching behind me, I pulled my pistol from its holster, held it firmly in my right hand, resting its reassuring weight across my left arm. In my left hand I held a small but powerful torch. There was no guarantee that whoever had left bits of a 'build your own human' kit scattered about the place was still around, but if they were, I wanted to be prepared.

The inside of the office was far more opulent than the tired old warehouse suggested, and my first step was cushioned by a thick, richly patterned carpet. The narrow beam of my torch flicked from side to side, glinting off several tall glass display cabinets, each filled with tasteful antiques. I wasn't particularly surprised. Any self-respecting crime lord owned at least one old warehouse, the older and more run down the better. The bricks and mortar equivalent of camouflage. The fancy office was all part of the package. If you're going to be spending time in the arse-end of nowhere then you might as well do so in comfort and style.

As my torchlight continued to work its way down the room, it settled on a large canvas. I don't know anything about art, but this looked expensive, a medley of broad colourful strokes in oils. Despite the roughness of each individual flourish, the overall effect managed to make me think of childhood holidays, days at the beach with the waves crashing in, leaving me laughing and soaked to the skin. Seeing as I can't remember my childhood, or anything before my arrival in the City, that was quite some feat.

This place seems to affect everyone in the same way. You can remember things at a conceptual level – childhood, fast food, favourite movies, all those staples of life. You know they exist, and even some of the details, but you can't remember experiencing them for yourself. It's pretty confusing and explains a lot about the way people in the City behave. Things that trigger phantom memories, that bring back feelings that we know we once had, they're worth something here.

I was so enamoured with the picture that I didn't pay as much attention to the rest of the room as I should have, so the first indication I got that things were wrong, or more specifically, even more wrong than before, was when I felt the thick carpet turn tacky underfoot.

Turning the beam downwards I checked out the carpet around my shoes. My first thought was that garish red was a bold interior design choice, followed very shortly by the realisation that the rest of the surrounding carpet was an off-white, and that the red was localised, and freshly added.

I knelt down and looked more closely, although I didn't really need to.

"Yup... blood," I muttered to myself. Whether it came from the unwilling donor of the eye and finger I had found outside remained to be seen, but there was a lot of it, leading to a large wooden desk at the far end of the room.

Whoever had left this much of their insides lying around wasn't likely to be alive now, but the spilt blood was still fresh enough to feel damp to the touch.

It might be that the large numbers of recently and violently dead people were making me especially edgy, but when I heard the gentle pad of footsteps behind me I turned and fired off a shot without stopping to think.

"Bloody hell, Pat! Watch what you're doing."

Standing just a few steps behind me, with a look that mixed disgust at standing paw deep in a blood-drenched carpet with the wide-eyed panic of having nearly been shot, was Samson.

"What the fuck, Samson? I could have killed you."

"I'm well aware of that, thanks," Samson replied, with a shudder. "I thought you might need some help, so, against my better judgement, I decided to follow you down here."

He lifted one paw fastidiously from the carpet and wrinkled his nose. "It's fair to say that I'm regretting that decision. I keep on stepping on bits of people... which is not nice."

"I appreciate the concern," I said, secretly touched that Samson, who was generally as self-centred as a gyroscope, had decided to risk at least one of his lives to help me out.

It took a moment for me to realise that he was no longer paying me any attention. Instead, his beady copper eyes were focused on the desk at the back of the room.

"Ughh," he said, "now that is particularly nasty... "

I turned back to face the desk, which was every bit as high quality as the other furniture in the room. Dark, rich mahogany, heavy with age and accumulated wealth. It was more a statement of intent than somewhere to shuffle papers. A way of saying, "I have power, money and privilege, and I know how to use them," without ever having to open your mouth.

It hadn't worked out that way for the occupant of the leather chair behind the desk. It seemed that all the power, money, and privilege in the world couldn't fully compensate for having your brain scooped out the back of your head. The mess that had been left behind was made horribly clear in the reflected image I could see in the large mirror on the rear wall.

Tearing my gaze away from the gruesome reflection, I looked back at the equally horrendous scene directly in front of me. It was the Dandy I remembered from Mrs Jones' club. Even with his face reduced to a blank mask and his eye sockets empty, he was easy enough to recognise. It's just that the last time I had seen him, he'd been in one piece. Now all that was left was a husk, hollowed out like a Halloween pumpkin, then placed back in his chair, his ridiculous cane still resting in a hand just beginning to clench with rigor mortis.

It was strange to finally find him like this. He had been the whispered terror pulling the strings of half the City, and I'd been convinced that he was behind Father Trent being torn from the world. Now I had found him, and the only thing left was a shell, one that had been posed for me to find.

I wasn't sure if this was supposed to be some kind of message, but other than 'don't fuck with me or I'll scoop out your insides like a cheap ice cream', I wasn't getting anything.

"So that's the Dandy, then. Not quite what I expected," Samson said in the background, but I paid him no attention.

I could have screamed in frustration, and very nearly did,

but ended up biting my tongue instead until I tasted blood. After everything I had gone through, trading in my one piece of genuine collateral, all I had found was a thoroughly dead end. I hadn't completely worked out how I was going to get the Dandy to answer my questions when I found him, but it was a moot point now, unless I suddenly added a bit of necromancy to my skill set.

"I don't suppose you left a handy note lying around, did you?" I asked the corpse. "Preferably one that explains what the hell is going on?"

I didn't get much back, just an extremely blank expression.

"Typical," I muttered, making my way round to his side of the desk. There didn't seem much chance that someone who had been so careful to completely eviscerate the Dandy would then leave any obvious clues for me to find, but I was feeling desperate.

About half an hour of feverish rummaging left me with a sum total of nothing. The desk drawers had been stripped bare, and while there was a lead running to the desktop suggesting that a laptop had been there at some point, it was long gone. Samson had got bored after the first few minutes and had left me to it, spending his time padding impatiently up and down and occasionally sticking his head back out the door.

"Expecting company?" I asked.

"Piss off, Pat. I don't want to be here any longer than necessary, so get a wriggle on."

Shrugging, I turned my attention back to the Dandy, and left Samson to his pacing.

The thoroughness, and lack of consideration for other people's property, put me in mind of the chaos I had found in my own office. Looking at the empty holes where the Dandy's eyes used to be added to my relief that neither Samson nor I had been around when the office had been hit.

"So, now what?" I asked the Dandy.

His rictus grin didn't help, although I got the sense he was mocking me.

"Last chance," I told him. "Whoever did this is messing with both of us."

Two empty eye sockets stared back at me accusingly.

"Fine. They may have messed with you a little more than me," I admitted.

"Can we get going?" Samson gave the back of my knee a gentle nudge with his nose. "No offence but this is getting a bit weird. I don't think he's going to be telling you... or anyone, anything... ever. Besides, sooner or later someone is going to come knocking and I don't want to be around when they do."

I knew Samson was right, and took one final look at the man who had been the undisputed King of the City, marvelling at how quickly things can change. The expensive suit was stained with blood and whatever other bodily fluids the Dandy had lost in his final moments, his hand still clasped around the ornate handle of his walking cane.

A thought occurred to me, one that I didn't dwell on for too long, in fear of once again getting ahead of myself. I reached forward and unpeeled the cold fingers one at a time, revealing the intricately carving at the head of the cane. Holding my breath, I slowly removed the walking stick from his clasp and turned it around under the light of my torch.

For a minute, I thought my instincts had been wrong, that there was nothing there to see, but then, as I completed a full rotation, a raised detail caught my eye in the torchlight. I ran my finger over it, but nothing happened. Pressing, twisting, and prodding proved equally fruitless. Thinking back to the layers of security at the door, I lifted the Dandy's thumb and pressed it down onto the raised section. I was rewarded with a satisfying click as a segment of the handle came loose. Although more decorative than most examples I had ever seen, what I was left holding was a memory stick of some kind.

"Maybe he still does have a couple of things to tell us after all," I told Samson, although he didn't look particularly convinced.

It only took a moment to stow the find in an inside pocket, replace the Dandy's hand around the cane and wipe the whole thing clean of any sign that I had been there. I wasn't keen to be tied to the death of the most powerful underworld figure in the City. I suspected that, if I were, then I would very quickly end up in jail, and things would go rapidly and terminally downhill from there.

Samson presented a rather different set of problems. On the plus side, I doubted that his prints were on file anywhere in the cesspit that passed for the City's police department. On the other hand, it was going to be hard to explain away a series of tiny, bloodied cat prints leading away from the scene of the Dandy's murder. After a brief but vigorous negotiation, I agreed to carry Samson as far as the exit and then never speak of the matter again.

I had a few things I wanted to follow up on before going back to the office, so when we got outside we headed our separate ways. After popping Samson down onto the pavement, and resisting a sudden urge to give him a tickle behind the ears, I settled instead for a nod of thanks.

Pain in the ass or not, it was good to have him in my corner.

CHAPTER 18

If you were to compile a list of all the things in the world that I am particularly bad at, anything to do with computers would rank close to the top, coming in just after sobriety, or understanding the more complex outliers of human emotion, so for the moment the memory stick wasn't much use to me. I was going to need some assistance to find out what secrets it held, presuming it held any at all.

There was at least one person I could think of who would be able to crack the memory pen open like a tiny metallic piñata.

Gaby knew her way around technology in a way I never would. I'd always thought of computers as an unnecessary layer of complication between me and the rest of the world. They might be incredibly clever and able to crunch more numbers than a steamroller in a dice factory, but I didn't trust them. At the end of the day, behind all the gadgetry there was still a human feeding it data, and humans were notoriously fallible. On the other hand, Gaby had always enjoyed an affinity with the shiny little bastards.

During the brief window of time when we had been working together and were still on speaking terms, her face would light up at the prospect of delving into the workings of some computer system or other, which made us a pretty good team. We would have been even more effective if we hadn't ended up fighting like starving cats in a bag, but for a while things had been close to perfect.

It might seem a bit churlish, or just really dumb of me to avoid asking her for help simply because of a complicated past, but of all the terrible things in the City – Daemons, Magick and psychopathic gang lords included – she was the one thing most likely to finish me.

It wasn't anything deliberate on her part. She was, as far as things go, a decent human being. Harsh, headstrong, and blunt to the point of rudeness, but ultimately decent. However, the thing you learn quickly about surviving in the City is that you will eventually lose everything you hold dear, no matter how tightly you grasp it.

That lesson had been painfully reiterated with the death of Trent. A good friend, whose company I had valued, whose conversation had whiled away many a dark evening, and whose untimely end had sent me down the dark path I was now locked into.

There had been a short and glorious time when losing Gaby would have been more than I could have lived with. I ended up losing her anyway, but it was long enough after those wonderful early days for the loss to be bearable.

Ruling her out left me with a pretty slim set of alternatives. There was only one other person I could think of, someone who was almost the exact opposite to Gaby. Sebastian was not a good or decent person, he and I didn't share any happy memories, and if I found out I would never see him again, I wouldn't shed a single tear. But he was, in his own way, competent.

He tended to hang out at the lower end of the upper-class clubs in the City. He wasn't rich enough, well connected enough, or smart enough to really fit in, but it didn't stop him trying. He had been dangling off the bottom of the social ladder for years, hanging on by the very tips of his expensively manicured fingernails. Despite this, he had slowly built up a reputation for being a reliable pair of hands when someone had a computer issue that they didn't want to draw too much attention to.

It wasn't the same as genuinely being part of the business set that he so desperately wished would accept him, but as long as he was useful then it kept his foot in the right doors, just enough to stop them from being slammed in his face.

***

The current hot ticket in town, away from Mrs Jones' club, which tended to be a little too raw for the starched collars of the business set, was the Libertarian. Like a lot of the fashionable clubs close to the centre, it had opened up a few weeks ago to great fanfare, would burn brightly for a few months, then fade into obscurity as the next big thing took centre stage. Chances are, that's where I would find Sebastian, circling a group of traders or bankers like a pilot fish swimming with a herd of sharks, picking over their scraps and dreaming that he was a shark too, rather than a glorified toothpick.

Luckily, I was already wearing my best suit, so I could go straight there without stopping to pretty myself up. It was admittedly quite heavily stained with a mixture of blood, oil, and general grime. I suspected that it might not smell that great either, but as my other suit was also bloodstained and had several large rips from where the Wrath Daemon had torn chunks out of me, I didn't have a lot of choice.

I could have tried some sort of distraction, used my wits or the last few remnants of Magick I could still feel lingering in my veins, but I'd had a hard couple of days. I settled for walking straight past the doorman like he wasn't even there.

Who knows, maybe the latest urban chic is the ragged vigilante look, because the guy hardly gave me a second glance.

The inside of the club was just how I imagined it to be, pretty much a match for the last five or six nightspots that had preceded it. Lots of shiny chrome, faux leather, and big mirrors, reflecting the desperate faces of the patrons straight back at them. The only respite came from the low lighting, meaning at least you couldn't see in too much detail just how sad and lonely your reflected self looked.

I'm pretty sure it was a deliberate move. Any partygoer seeing clearly just how big the bags under their eyes had got would pack it in after one drink, promising themselves an early night and a week or two of sensible living, but the murky half-light was just enough to hide the worst and keep them hanging on for one more round.

Away from the bar, there were clusters of seats set against the walls, each housing a microcosm of the business community.

In one there were the sharp suits and sharper conversation of the City's lawyers and solicitors. There's plenty of money to be made feeding and then dampening down the flames of legal dispute, and this was one of the places where they spent it.

The next booth was crammed with traders at the start of brief, glittering careers. A few of them would make it through the year, start making the really big money, land a corner office and a semi-permanent place on the board. Most wouldn't, burning out as quickly as the expensive smokes they favoured.

Sebastian wasn't with either of the first two groups, although it wasn't a major surprise. The lawyers were too smart and the traders too keen on showing off their wealth. Then I spotted him. A couple of tables further along there was a small group of arty types, hanging out after a big night in the Theatre District. I could imagine Sebastian was having a great old time listening in on all their excitable chatter, imagining himself as part of their tempestuous, exciting lives. The fact that none of them cared whether he was there or not didn't seem to matter.

He was doing what he did ninety per cent of the time, which was to laugh at whatever his new circle of so-called friends were saying as if it was the funniest thing he'd ever heard. No-one was paying him any attention, but you had to give him points for effort. If ass-kissing was a sport, Sebastian would be a serious gold medal contender. He was so busy concentrating on buttering up his buddies that he didn't spot me until I was right next to him, which, considering the way I looked, was pretty impressive.

When he did see me, his face dropped and the latest bull-shit laugh died as it left his lips, turning into more of a strangled gurgle.

"Judas."

It was only my name, but the way he said it summed up exactly how Sebastian felt about seeing me. It had been a few months since the last time I had worked with him, and I was guessing he didn't remember it with as much fondness as I did. Probably it was because I hadn't paid him, and he'd ended up getting his nose broken by a very disappointed client. On the other hand, if I hadn't been there, he would have suffered a lot more than a broken nose.

"Hi, Sebastian, good to see you again," I said, just loud enough to pierce the little bubble of conversation around the table. A couple of the arty types were interested enough to stop mid-sentence and give me a proper look. I would imagine they didn't often get accosted by a six-foot-something private eye wearing a blood-stained jacket and with half his face burned to a crisp, so I was a novelty if nothing else.

Meanwhile, Sebastian was suffering a serious case of 'be careful what you wish for'. After having spent the last few hours desperate to be noticed, now he and I were the centre of attention, and it was obviously not quite the experience he had been dreaming of.

He was smart enough to know that I wasn't going anywhere and nodded to a couple of empty stools by the bar.

"You're buying," he told me, before I had even taken my seat.

"Fair enough, what's your poison?"

He took a minute to deliberately scan the top shelf of the bar, presumably looking for something really expensive, and settled on a fancy looking single malt. It was a much better choice than I had expected and cost five times as much as I would normally be comfortable paying.

"So, to what do I owe this pleasure?" He took a sip of his drink, which was making me thirsty just watching.

"I need access to whatever is stored on this." I held up the memory stick, the metal surface glinting with flashes of pink and green, reflected neon from the strip lights running around the top of the bar.

Sebastian didn't say anything, just held out his hand. Recent events had added to my already considerable trust issues, but the stick was useless to me in its current state, so I handed it across. He turned it over a couple of times, humming tunelessly to himself under his breath. Whatever else he was, he knew his tech, and I could tell that he was itching to know what I'd brought him.

"Wait here," he told me, as he wandered back over to the booth to collect a small shoulder bag. Like most of the things he owned, it was designer and more expensive than he could probably afford. Laying the bag on the bar, he took out a small laptop, which he rested on his knees, swivelling around on his stool to face me, and popped the memory stick into a port on its side.

"Before I look at this," he said, fixing me with his pale blue eyes, his fingers pausing just above the keyboard, "I have a couple of questions."

"Go ahead."

"Firstly, is there anything on this that's going to land me in the shit?" He unconsciously readjusted his glasses as he spoke, running his finger across the spot where the bones of his nose had reset slightly out of line.

"Second, what's the content of this little stick worth to you? You still owe me for the last piece of work you brought my way. To be clear, I don't like you, I'm not a charity, and I don't like being dicked around."

Both questions were fair, and not ones that I was in a position to answer honestly. I was pretty sure that if I told him that the memory stick had recently been removed from the corpse of the City's biggest gang lord and that the expensive whisky I had just brought him was as far as my finances were going to stretch, then he would tell me exactly where I could shove it.

I decided to start with the easier of the two. "I'm not going to be able to pay you upfront, but…"

Sebastian's eyes had already narrowed, so I pressed on before he could hand the stick back.

"…but, what's on that stick is worth a lot, a small fortune to the right people, and you'll get your cut."

His gaze was still suspicious, but I was pretty sure I'd got him hooked. As well as an overwhelming desire to better his social standing, Sebastian had a blind spot when it came to gambling. It was the reason, outside of the expensive designer wear and fancy skincare regime, why he was always up to his neck in debt. It was also the only reason why he'd ever agreed to work with me in the past. His natural distaste for my grubby attire and grubbier work had been outweighed by a pressing need to pay back serious sums of money to even more serious lenders. That had made the fact that I ended up not paying him on our last job very disappointing for everyone involved.

I didn't try to answer the first part of his question, the whole 'landing him in the shit' thing, because there was absolutely no way to put a positive spin on it. The best I could do was to get him to crack whatever security was on the memory stick, take it far, far away, and swear with my dying breath that we'd never met. Fortunately, the mention of a small fortune had taken all of his attention, and I could see he was already mentally planning what to do with his share as he began to tap away on the compact keyboard.

I ordered a coffee while he did his stuff. It didn't come anywhere close to scratching the itch I had for one of the single malts that Sebastian was enjoying at my expense, but I needed to keep a clear head. Plus, I was already pumped so full of painkillers that I rattled when I walked. Topping them off with whisky would either make me very sleepy or very fighty, neither of which was going to help.

"Shit… oh shit, shit, shit, fuck, shitting, fucking shit!"

Even in the dingy half-light of the club, Sebastian's face had gone very pale.

"Something wrong?"

"You know what's wrong, you son of a bitch," he growled. "This is full of the Dandy's files… shit, shit, shit, I'm a dead man just for looking at this."

I made a vaguely calming motion, which achieved absolutely nothing. Sebastian was still too busy going through a long and impressive list of expletives, most of which referenced me in one way or another.

"And why the bloody hell did you get me to look at it here? It's not exactly private," he added, gesturing feverishly around him. On that front at least, he had nothing to worry about. Clubs like this attracted one type of person – ambitious, successful, wealthy, and with zero interest in anyone else.

"Let's walk and talk," I said, pushing myself up from my stool. "There's a bit of background you might find enlightening."

It wasn't all that inspiring, but a drowning man will clutch a matchstick if there's nothing else around to keep him afloat.

"Fine," Sebastian grunted, folding the laptop and jamming it back into his shoulder bag.

I'm a pretty tall guy, with a long stride, but I had to hustle to keep up with Sebastian's panicky half-run as we left the club and re-entered the chill of the night air.

"This better be good," he said as soon as we were outside. "You've got two minutes and then I am going to have to start running. I would have suggested you do the same, but I frankly wouldn't give a damn if the Dandy catches up with you."

"That's the thing," I replied. "The Dandy won't be coming for me, you, or anyone else. Not now, not ever again."

"I'm not sure I'm liking the sound of this any better."

"It's the truth," I told him. "The Dandy is gone… not by my hand," I added, seeing the look Sebastian was giving me. "It's his memory stick, true enough, but he's not around, and it looked like a lot of his best boys went down with him."

I didn't mention the fact that Cain was still around and presumably would be looking to avenge his boss's untimely and messy death. Sebastian's mental state was fragile enough as it was.

"What it does mean is that no-one is looking for this… yet, and whatever it was that the Dandy wanted to keep so close is going to be worth more than its weight in gold, or diamonds, or whatever."

It was enough to stop Sebastian in his tracks, even if only for a moment. Avarice was a strong motivation, even when it was balanced by fear. He was tapping his fingers against the supple leather of his bag, nervous but thinking, weighing options.

"If I open this up for you, I don't want to see you or it ever again. Whatever value there is in it, you can transfer me my share, anonymously."

It was the false bravado of a man with no options. Sebastian was smart enough to know that his card had been marked as soon as he had touched the pen drive. Safe to say I had burned my bridges with him for good this time. I just hoped that whatever the Dandy had been hiding away was worthwhile, something that would finally make some sense. If there was actually something on there worth a bit of cash... well, that was a bonus.

"Give me a couple of hours. I'll call you when it's done."

He didn't wait for my answer, just stalked off into the darkness of the night.

Seeing as I still had a few hours to myself, I left the expensive neon of the club behind and headed for an altogether nastier part of the City. Sooner or later, I was going to have to face Cain again. Painful experience had taught me that in a fair fight I wouldn't stand a chance, so it seemed like a good idea to level the playing field a little.

I might not be able to do much about the physical advantages that Cain enjoyed, and the guy could absorb so much damage that I would likely burn myself out before I could finish the bastard with Magick, but I could try to make sure that, when I faced him next time, I'd still enjoy a few home-turf advantages.

I spent a few hours at an old, abandoned construction site that had caught my eye a few nights before, putting some surprises together, things I hoped might give me an edge... if I could lure Cain across town. Some people might call it cheating, and they'd probably be right. But the bottom line is that the world would be better off without Cain, and if stacking the deck in my favour is the only way to achieve that, then that's what I'll do.

CHAPTER 19

Sebastian still hadn't called by the following morning, and I was beginning to seriously regret handing him the memory stick. I had risked everything I had left to get hold of it, and then given it to someone who had every reason to hate me. I could only blame a combination of sleep deprivation, blood loss, and a genetic predisposition towards making poor choices.

Samson hadn't been so forgiving. When he heard what I'd done, he didn't waste any time telling me in no uncertain terms that I should have gone to Gaby, and that I was a stupid prick for trusting someone like Sebastian.

"I shouldn't have left you to sort things out without me," he said, with a particularly scathing look. "You're the kind of self-destructive dickhead who'd play Russian Roulette with a bullet in every chamber."

I didn't argue. Firstly, because I was too tired to think of a reasonable defence, and second, because Samson had a pretty solid point. Chances were, Sebastian had either tried to sell the memory stick or he'd gone into hiding. Then there was the third option, which was that Cain had already caught up with him and Sebastian was now extremely dead.

I had just settled on the third option as being the most likely, when the office phone chirruped at me.

"Judas... Judas, is that you?" It was Sebastian, but all the false bravado from the previous evening had gone completely from his voice. He sounded exhausted and very, very scared.

"I found a way into the rest of the files on that memory stick... it took longer than I thought... the security was tight as hell."

The call fell silent for a few seconds.

"And?"

"I've sent it back across to your office by courier. I don't want anything from you or anything that's on that cursed thing. No amount of money's worth the shit you've dragged me into."

There was a buzz as the line went dead.

The courier arrived a few minutes later, although that was an overly complimentary description. It was just some kid that Sebastian had found and handed a bit of coin to. It was a smart enough move, he didn't have to worry about handing over any details, keeping the link between us as fuzzy as possible.

I have to admit, my hands were shaking as I slotted the drive back into my computer. A lot was riding on whatever it contained, and judging from how freaked out Sebastian had sounded, there was definitely something on there. I just had to hope that it was something that I would be able to use.

Whatever else the Dandy might have been, he kept his filing nice and tidy. I guess that's why I never progressed from backstreet private eye to terrifying gang lord. I'm too disorganised. There were just two folders on the drive, the first full of spreadsheet files that meant nothing to me. They might have held the secrets to all of the Dandy's finances, but I wasn't savvy enough to know. The second folder was a bit more straightforward, a single video file. I pressed play and settled back.

It looked like it was the feed from the Dandy's security system at the warehouse, and from the date and timestamp in the lower right hand of the picture, it was from earlier in the same day I had broken in. The camera was focused on the interior of the Dandy's office, although with the notable difference that the Dandy was still moving around, and with the inside of his head intact.

For a few minutes, nothing much happened. The guy was

just sat there, tapping away on his computer keyboard now and then, looking more like a bored office worker than a kingpin of crime, playing a few rounds of solitaire to while away the hours. I guess it's not the glamourous life I had imagined. There were no armed guards driving miniature golf buggies, no glamourous assistants, and no bank of monitors showing his various dastardly schemes being carried out. There wasn't even a shark tank.

Just as I was reaching for the fast forward, a second figure entered the office, shuffling his way across the other side of the desk, although frustratingly with his back to the camera. "Pretty crappy security system," I muttered at the digitised version of the Dandy. I don't think he heard me, what with him being a video recording, but the fact that he was dead suggested I was right.

The Dandy and his guest seemed to know one another. There was a handshake, some drinks, some chat, all very friendly. An envelope passed from the visitor to the Dandy, which vanished almost immediately into one of the drawers of the heavy desk. Then a final handshake and the figure rose and turned to leave the office.

I pressed pause and stared. The resolution, even at a distance, was good enough to pick out the features on the visitor's face. It was one that I recognised and had seen only recently. There was no mistaking the cold eyes, beaked nose, and general miserable expression of Augustus Creech.

Making a mental note to follow up on Creech, I checked the time on the video. There were still a couple of hours of footage to go, so I poured myself a strong coffee, grabbed a sandwich and settled in.

The rest of the footage confirmed what the start had suggested. The majority of the Dandy's last day had been completely underwhelming. The meeting with Creech was definitely the highlight, after which he had spent the remainder sat at his desk. Then, just as I thought I'd wasted the last couple of hours, all hell broke loose on the screen.

The first sign that something was wrong was when the Dandy suddenly leant forward to stare intently at the screen in front of him. Then he snatched at the phone on his desk and barked something into it. The video feed didn't appear to include any sound but judging by the mess I had found when I had broken into his office, I could hazard a guess at the conversation taking place.

Even before he had finished his call there was a flurry of movement, two figures running into the room, big guys in expensive suits, packing serious-looking firepower. They squared up in front of the Dandy's desk, turning to face the doorway and signalling for the Dandy to stay behind them. Whilst their professionalism was admirable, their effectiveness was less impressive, with first one then the other collapsing within seconds of entering the room. I couldn't make out what had taken them out, but the second bodyguard ended up minus most of his head, which looked like it exploded from the inside out, and which also explained why I had found so much blood on the office floor.

Still seated, apparently stunned by the sudden turn of events, the Dandy was just starting to reach for something in the drawer of his desk when the picture cut out, leaving me looking at a blank screen.

Although the footage had ended at that point, I knew well enough how things were going to end, with the Dandy scooped empty, but that didn't answer the big question of who was responsible. I had risked plenty to see what secrets the Dandy had been keeping, and all I knew was that Creech had been to see him a few hours before he died.

It wasn't much to go on. Wondering if I had missed something, I rewound the video back to Creech's arrival and took another look. For most of the conversation, the Dandy's face wasn't at an angle where I could even guess what he was saying. Then, just before Creech passed him the envelope, I caught a break. The Dandy leant back in his seat as he said something, meaning I got a clear look at his mouth. I replayed the section a few times, tracking the footage back and forth over and over. Without sound, it was hard to be sure, but it looked like he was saying something about 'the Elevator'.

I'm not an expert lipreader, so it could have been something completely different, but once that thought got into my head it was impossible for me to think of anything else. It wasn't exactly the silver bullet I might have been hoping for, but seeing as I had already followed the trail back to the Elevator once before, there seemed no harm in trying again. Besides, Barbara was probably missing me by now.

CHAPTER 20

"You again."

"Me again," I admitted, realising that Barbara was unlikely to believe I was anyone else.

"And..."

A lesser man would have given up there and then. She had managed to squeeze more disappointment, apathy, and general negativity into that one word than you could imagine was possible. Fortunately, I had already reached rock bottom as far as self-esteem goes.

"Just needed a quick favour, then I'll be out of your hair."

"That's what you said last time, Judas," she sighed, giving her glasses a particularly aggressive polish. The fact that she had led straight away with 'Judas' rather than 'Pat' wasn't promising, but I pressed ahead anyway.

"It's about the book again... or specifically, who's scheduled for the Elevator."

"It's private, Judas, you know that. Same as I told you last time."

"I know, and same as last time I don't need to see the book. Just... look up another name for me and let me know if there's something odd going on... please?"

She didn't exactly look delighted, but there was a glimmer in the corner of her eye that made me think she was going to help. Tough nut that she was, Barbara hated anything that messed with the orderly way the Elevator went about its strange business. She might not want to help me out, but the chance that something could disrupt her carefully managed routine was an itch she would eventually have to scratch.

"Fine. One name… and then you can leave."

"Barbara, you're the best. The name I'm looking for is Creech… Augustus Creech."

Barbara nodded, waved me away from the desk, and then pulled the book out from its cubbyhole.

"That's odd," Barbara muttered, poring over the huge, heavy pages of the ledger. "His name is in here right where it should be, but…" she pointed to an entry about two-thirds of the way down.

Whatever it was, it had shaken her enough to let me take a look, so I leaned in to see what had caught her attention.

There he was, Augustus Creech, the name picked out in neat, handwritten copperplate. In the next column was a date, just a couple of days away, which again wasn't unusual. Lots of the names had dates by them, but I managed to fight the instinct to check any of the others. It might be tempting to know the future, but most of the time it's a burden you really don't want.

What was unusual was that the date by his name had been crossed out and a small handwritten addendum added. Just a single word. 'Deferred.'

"What does that mean?" I asked, still thrown off balance by the sight of Barbara looking puzzled. Barbara never looked puzzled, not ever.

"It doesn't happen often," she replied, pushing the ledger away with an annoyed exhalation. "But very, very rarely there are special circumstances where someone's departure date gets postponed. It creates a load of paperwork and most of the time it only changes things by a few days."

"So, when has his departure been deferred to?" I asked, although I had a growing feeling of certainty that was making itself known deep in my guts. Either that, or I was developing an ulcer.

"That's the strangest thing of all," Barbara said, scanning up and down the page with one well-manicured finger. "There is no date... which can't be right, there's always a date."

She gave another exasperated sigh, before slamming the ledger closed, hitting me with a gust of air that tasted of old paper and something else that was impossible to identify.

I took that as my cue to leave. Much as I enjoyed spending time with Barbara, I knew it wouldn't be long before she was looking down her impressively long nose at me again, fingers itching to call security, even if only for old times' sake.

As I walked out under the cold night sky, I took one final look back at the reception desk picked out in a pool of light amid the surrounding blackness and realised that I had never seen Barbara anywhere except sat behind that desk. I wasn't even sure that she existed from the waist down.

My brain took a firm step back at that point. Thinking about Barbara below the waist was not a route it was willing to go down. For a start, I was pretty sure that somehow she'd know... and she would not be happy.

What I did know was that my only paying client was involved in whatever was going on, up to his miserable, cold-fish eyeballs. My hunch about his conversation with the Dandy had turned out to be right. Somehow, he had managed to get his well-deserved trip in the Elevator deferred.

It's a rule of mine never to mess with my clients. It helps to keep business clean and easy, and in my line of work, word of mouth and personal recommendations go a long way. However, it's also a rule of mine not to allow morally bankrupt assholes to murder my friends, have my offices trashed, or mess with the nature of reality, so I was at a bit of an impasse.

I wasn't convinced that Creech was behind everything

that had gone down over the last few days. On the other hand, I knew where he lived and now I had a pretty good reason to pay him a house call. If nothing else, he was a rung on whatever slippery ladder I was intent on climbing.

CHAPTER 21

This time I didn't bother calling ahead. I had a strong feeling that Creech wouldn't be pleased to see me. He didn't seem like the kind of guy to let his guard down at the best of times, and I was certain that word of the Dandy's untimely demise would have reached him by now. His home and office were going to be locked up pretty tight, and that was only if he hadn't already made for some bolthole or another.

My right shoulder and arm were hurting like hell, a clear signal that I should be resting up somewhere comfortable and paying back the cost of the Magick I had been using over the last couple of days. I knew it was only going to get worse, but I didn't have the luxury of time, and the regular pain killers I had been shovelling down weren't even coming close to taking the edge off.

Before I called in on Creech there were a couple of things I needed to do. First, I stopped off at the office. Samson was asleep, and for once I decided to leave him in peace. His life had been pretty messed up recently, and like it or not, I knew it was my fault. I did leave him a short note, basically telling him to stay inside, keep the door locked, and not be too surprised if he never saw me again. A little melodramatic, maybe, but it was hard to see how I was going to navigate my way through this one and still come out alive at the end.

That just left enough time to drop into a backstreet pharmacy I knew, where they were a little more liberal than most with their medication, where I splashed out on the very strongest pills they had hidden away under the counter. They weren't cheap, and the side-effects were worryingly open-ended, but at least I could keep moving.

***

The grounds of Creech's place were deserted when I arrived. My car was still stuck up near the hospital, so I had treated myself to a taxi to get most of the way there.

The gates were very firmly closed, and I was certain the walls would have a few nasty tricks up their sleeves for any unsuspecting intruders foolish enough to attempt climbing them. I had no intention of even trying. Years of digging into people's private lives and exhuming their most deeply buried secrets had taught me a lot about getting into secure places, and Creech's mansion was no different.

I knew for a fact that Mrs Creech had been out earlier in the day and hadn't yet returned. I also knew that Creech was jealous enough to want to keep her close, especially when the shit was well and truly en route to the fan, and would have called her back to the mansion. So, rather than try to open the gates myself, I hunkered down and waited for someone to open them for me.

I had been waiting just over an hour, the restless air of the gathering dusk giving way to the refined stillness of the night, when I spotted the headlamps of her car. She wouldn't be driving herself, so I had to hope that whoever it was had some sort of basic moral code, otherwise the next part of my plan wouldn't end well.

As the 4 x 4 drew close to the gates, its headlamps picked out the bundle of rags I had carefully placed a little earlier. They were big enough to give any driver a momentary pause and human enough in size and shape to make most people stop and check whether they had been about to run someone down.

For a minute, I thought the car was just going to keep driving. Presumably, Creech had given his guys strict instructions to return straight away, not stopping for anything, but at the last moment the car squealed to a halt, just a few metres from the scrappy pile of material.

A moment later, the driver's door popped open and someone emerged. She was big and tough-looking, apparently doubling as Mrs Creech's security as well as being her chauffeuse.

"Stay in the car, please, ma'am," she called back over her shoulder, before advancing on the rags, her sidearm drawn. It was a tricky position, and I sympathised with her. She could tell something was up, but it looked like she was on her own, and she had to try and keep an eye on the blockage in the road, as well as looking out for any potential ambush or secondary danger. She had a flashlight in her other hand, and after focusing for a few seconds on the rags, she swept either side of the SUV. I was well hidden behind the deep, thick scrub at the roadside, but I still held my breath as the light bled around the edges of my hiding place.

As soon as it passed, I was on the move, staying low and quiet. By now the driver had reached the rags and was giving them a tentative poke with her shoe, which meant I was nearly out of time. Wishing myself luck, I rolled under the side of the vehicle, placing myself bang in the centre and gripped tightly onto the most substantial looking part of the skidpan. I wouldn't have managed to get away with it if she had been using anything with a lower wheelbase, but I'd done my homework and knew there was just enough space.

Moments later, the driver was back in her seat, having cleared from the road the mix of fabric and other rubbish I had used. It was a random enough selection to make it feasible that it was there by accident, although unlikely, and certainly suspicious enough to set a few internal alarm bells ringing.

Fortunately, the drive from the gate to the large garage block was short enough for my cobbled-together breaking and entering suit to hold together. I had no desire to have my back turned into corned beef as I was dragged along the tarmac and had lined the back of my jacket with a layer of steel mesh, which more or less did the job for the few seconds it needed to.

Even so, I left it a couple of minutes, well after the heavy footsteps of the driver and the lighter tip-tap of Mrs Creech's designer heels had left the garage, before clambering out from under the vehicle and checking myself over.

The SUV was parked up alongside a smaller, sportier number, which I guessed was Mrs Creech's weekend drive. Her husband didn't look like the convertible two-seater type, nor did he look like someone who drove for pleasure. To be honest, I wasn't sure he did anything for pleasure – even his wife seemed more of a status symbol than someone whose company he actually enjoyed.

The security that had sealed the exterior of the sprawling house tight like a clam hadn't extended to the interior doors. Presumably, Creech's security detail had confidence in the protection afforded by the high walls and gates, as the door between the garage and the main house was still open.

The garage connected into a section of the mansion I hadn't seen before, a wide corridor with a pair of doorways to each side. The first was the security hub for the building. I could hear the muted mutter of voices, one male, one female, with the woman's voice recognisable as the driver.

In movies, the hero would bust into the security office and take out the guards in a couple of smooth moves. I didn't even consider trying.

Firstly, this isn't a movie, which means that all sorts of unforeseen things could crop up and mess with me. Secondly, the security detail was likely to consist of regular rent-a-cop types, so if I could avoid a situation where someone might end up dead, then I would. Last of all, there was no guarantee that the person ending up dead wouldn't be me, and I had a few things I still wanted to do with my life. See a beautiful sunset with someone I love, finally learn to play an instrument, rip Cain's head off and shove it up his arse... a pretty regular bucket list.

So, instead of busting my way into the office, I just walked past, taking care to be quiet. It meant that I was going to have to keep my eyes peeled for cameras, but I was hoping that the inside of the house wouldn't be as well covered as the outside, with Creech unlikely to want the interior workings of his office, bedrooms or bathrooms caught on camera.

The doorway at the far end of the corridor opened up into the main atrium and the part of the house I was familiar with, from my previous visits. The only difference was that the lights were dimmed, and I wasn't being escorted by a stern, bespectacled housekeeper. From memory, Creech's office was the third door along the first-floor landing. There was light spilling out from under the door, which was no major surprise. Creech struck me as being one for working late.

Getting to the door without being spotted was going to take a bit of work. While Creech might want to maintain his privacy in other areas of the house, I was certain the hallway and stairs would be well covered by security. Hunkering down in the shadows of the corridor, I took a minute to scan around the expansive walls and ceiling until I spotted the tell-tale glass domes of a couple of cameras.

***

It was times like this when Merle's lessons came in handy, much as I hate to admit it. I might bitch about the guy, and the toll that Magick takes on me each time I use it, but truth be told, it's saved my ass more times than I care to mention.

Moving fast was one of the last tricks that Merle had taught me, even though it was pretty much the first one I had ever seen him do, back when we bumped into each other. I was fascinated to know how he'd managed to take out Frank and end up behind Dave, quicker than I could blink.

Turns out he left it till the end because it was bloody hard to learn. Same as all the other tricks and apparent shortcuts that Magick opened the door to, there was a hefty price tag attached to all that convenience.

You know the feeling you get on a rollercoaster, just as you drop over the edge of the biggest dip and accelerate downwards, the g-force pressing you back into your seat, flapping your cheeks and pushing your eyes back in their sockets? Well, the sensation of pushing your way through the still air is a bit like that, but much, much worse.

According to Merle, a true master of the arts can weave their way through that resistance, letting it run off their skin like rain, but I'm not a master, far from it. So, when I move fast, I end up battering my way through the air, like a bull charging through a series of concrete walls.

I had spent countless hours working through Merle's fun little training exercises, standing at one end of a long room, as he threw a ball into the air at the other, tasking me to catch it before it hit the ground.

In the first dozen or so attempts, I hadn't even managed to take one step, too busy concentrating on the feeling of the air around me to make any actual progress. Then something clicked, and I found my way. It still felt like I was swimming underwater, the air thick and clammy, refusing to let go of my skin, dragging me back every time I tried even the smallest of steps, but it was a start.

It must have been at least a week before I managed to get to the far end of the room without giving up, and another week until I was competent enough to catch the ball before it hit the ground. I remember laying there, completely exhausted but clutching the ball triumphantly in one hand. Merle was standing there, impassive as always, one hand behind his back.

"Again," he'd say, holding out his hand for the ball and then gesturing me back to my starting point at the far end of the room.

He threw the ball into the air and I started towards him, eyes focused on the sight of the ball hanging between us like a miniature sun. It definitely felt easier, despite my aching limbs, and I got halfway across the room before the ball had even started to drop.

Then Merle brought his other hand from behind his back, which, it turned out, was holding a selection of very sharp-looking knives. He gave me a wink, then threw them into the air, filling the space between me and the ball with a series of shiny metallic death-traps. He didn't smile exactly, but I got the impression he was genuinely enjoying himself for the first time that day.

***

I'm still not exactly a master of the craft, but even so, compared to trying to dodge my way through a shower of levitating knives, crossing a largely empty hallway was a cakewalk. It was possible that the cameras might pick up a slight disturbance in the air as I passed, but nothing that would be recognisable as a person. I inhaled deeply, then launched myself across the hallway and up the stairs, not letting that breath escape until I was outside the door to Creech's office.

I allowed myself a minute. My technique might have improved over time, but I still felt like I'd just ascended the north face of the Eiger, rather than walk up a few stairs.

Once my breathing had slowed back down to something close to normal, and I was certain I wasn't bleeding from anywhere new, I pulled out my gun, knocked politely, and opened the door.

Immediately, I felt an unwelcome sense of déjà vu, and it wasn't the fact that I'd only been in this office not that many hours ago – that wouldn't class as déjà vu, it's just going somewhere twice. It was more the fact that the scene I was met with was almost identical to what I'd found in the Dandy's warehouse.

Creech was sat behind his desk, in the exact same spot as the last time I had seen him, the major difference being he was now missing most of the inside of his head, scooped empty just like the Dandy.

Considering the horror of what must have happened in the room, he was sat in a remarkably peaceful pose, fingers steepled in front of his beak-like nose as if he was puzzling his way through a particularly complex problem. Nor was there the mess of blood and guts that I'd waded through at the warehouse. Whatever had happened here had been quick, quiet, and sudden.

It looked like I had run into another dead end. I didn't feel any sympathy for the husk perched over his desk. He was undoubtedly a horrible old bastard who should have gone down in the Elevator a good few years ago, but I was growing increasingly angry that someone was managing to stay one step ahead of me, killing all my suspects before I could speak to them.

CHAPTER 22

Questioning Creech was clearly off the agenda now, leaving me short of options. Despite that, things were beginning to click. I could finally see the edge of the jigsaw, and it wasn't pretty. In one of the corners there was Eve, scheduled for an untimely descent in the Elevator, then in another, there was Father Trent, killed before he could take his final journey. The two things were related, but I'd just been too wrapped up in my own misery to realise. Then there was the ledger and the 'deferment' of Creech's trip, which filled in at least one of the bottom corners.

Eve and Creech were two opposite ends of the same puzzle. One who didn't deserve to go down suddenly destined for a terminal trip in the Elevator, the other – who had earned that final judgement – suddenly cut loose.

Someone had been playing fast and loose with the destiny of others. Trading places, swapping the fate of good people with the most rotten individuals in the City, desperate to cheat their way out of their inevitable trip downtown. Whoever was running all of this had to be phenomenally well connected, and up to the point when I found him dead, my money had been on the Dandy.

Now, it looked like someone was covering their trail. Killing anyone who could link back to whoever was sitting right at the top of the chain, which had to mean I was close to making a breakthrough. Taking out the Dandy was no mean feat, and it smacked of desperation. The problem was, I still didn't know enough to fill in the rest of the picture, and sooner or later, whoever had come knocking for the Dandy would come for me.

A more immediate problem was the fact that I had just broken into the office of a very dead, very unpleasant old man. Even worse than that, I had just come from the Dandy's warehouse, which also contained a higher-than-average number of corpses. Anyone who had been keeping tabs on my recent movements could very easily jump to the wrong conclusions.

The feverish ticking of my mind was interrupted by a gentle cough.

"Good evening, Mr Judas,"

The voice from just behind me was soft and familiar. One that I recognised from smoky late nights in the Club, although the rough edges had been sanded smooth.

Mrs Creech was standing just inside the open doorway to the office, looking a little paler than usual, but still amazingly composed for someone who had just walked in on the mutilated remains of her dear old hubby.

She had changed out of her glamourous 'going out' clothes into something far more casual and comfy. The dress had been swapped out for loungewear and the heels traded for expensive sneakers, which had presumably helped her approach me so quietly. Her only nods to glamour were a small white-gold brooch in the shape of a bird, and a wristwatch that probably cost more than I'd earn in a year.

"Seems like we both find ourselves in rather an unusual position," she said, breaking the uncomfortable silence. It was a strange opening line, but it could have been a lot worse. Believe me, you haven't even come close to experiencing awkward until you've been discovered standing over the body of a recently eviscerated old man, by the wife you have been professionally stalking for the last couple of weeks.

"I think we should talk," she continued, before darting a disparaging look at the remains of her husband, "but perhaps in a different room."

I wasn't exactly sure where this was going, I just had to hope it wasn't somewhere too unpleasant. It's not like there were any more attractive options. I could run, which would work for about as long as it took for Mrs Creech to call the authorities, or I could kill her, which seemed like a bit of an over-reaction.

Wasting no time, Mrs Creech led me along the landing to another set of grand doors, which opened up into a fairly small, but still impressive, library. The room appeared to have originally been a bedroom, but now the walls to either side were lined with fitted bookshelves, with a couple of large comfy wing-back chairs set close to the window. Unlike the sets of expensive leatherbound volumes in the office, at least some of the books appeared to have been read. It looked like a recent change, and I wondered if this was one of the rooms where Mrs Creech had stamped a little of her personality on the place.

"Sit… please," Mrs Creech indicated one of the wingbacks and took a seat in the other.

The armchair was comfortable, and it was tempting to let that comfort envelop me, the exhaustion I had been fighting off for the last couple of days threatening to overwhelm me completely, but I fought the urge to sink back in the seat and leaned forward instead, deliberately making myself as uncomfortable as possible. However, I wasn't quite so committed to discomfort as to refuse the glass of whisky being poured from a cut glass decanter.

"So, what the hell happened here?" I asked, deciding it was time to ask a few questions of my own. "No offence, Mrs Creech, but you don't seem all that shook up."

She gave me a long, calculating look, before answering.

"First thing, you can call me Susanna. I don't think I'll be keeping the Creech name any longer than I need to. Second, Augustus got what he deserved. He was about the nastiest man I ever had the misfortune to know. And I've met my fair share of complete bastards in my time."

As she spoke, her voice became increasingly bitter, and although she maintained an aura of cool composure, I could sense the turmoil raging underneath, a snow globe of whirling emotion underneath her glassy exterior.

Considering that what was left of Mr Creech had the insides of its head missing, 'got what he deserved' was a pretty harsh judgement. Whatever had gone on between the two of them had been enough to cement an intensity of icy hatred that I had rarely witnessed, and I'm speaking as someone who has profited from fractured and broken relationships for a large part of my working life.

Despite the emotion eddying beneath her words, she remained calm, even managing to look vaguely relaxed. I thought back to the woman I had known years before, working the floor of Mrs Jones' Club, a chameleon changing into whatever she needed to be in that moment. She had always been a good actress, and someone who had less experience with the grubbier side of human emotion may have even fallen for her current 'couldn't give a damn' show, but I wasn't buying it.

"You haven't answered my question, what happened here? I needed to speak to your husband, and it's looking like he won't be answering anyone's questions."

"He was fine when I left earlier today," she said, one hand toying subconsciously with her brooch, "… although there was something on his mind. I didn't think it was possible for him to be scared, but he was… discomforted."

I didn't say anything, just let the silence hang there like a big black hole, waiting to be filled. It's a remarkably effective technique. Some people just can't deal with the quiet. They feel compelled to fill it, and can be a little thoughtless about what they fill it with. Susanna was as sharp as they come, but composed exterior or not, she had got caught up in something terrible and it had left her wanting to talk. So I let her.

"He wouldn't tell me what it was, just that he had an important deal he was finalising. He had been working on it for the last couple of months, and whatever it was must have been big, because he was pulling together as much money as he could lay his hands on, closing down accounts. To be honest, I don't even know if there is enough left to keep paying for this place."

I thought back to the moment captured on the Dandy's video feed, Creech handing over his envelope, presumably payment for the 'deferment' that had so confused Barbara. I wondered how much it cost to sidestep your fate these days. Whatever it had been, Creech must have felt it was worth it, staving off his inevitable trip in the Elevator for just a little while longer. Shame for him that things hadn't turned out quite as he'd planned.

It seemed Mrs Creech hadn't been privy to all the details of her husband's schemes, and I wasn't sure that sharing what I knew was going to help matters. I could have felt sorry for her, but she'd made a choice when she had tied herself to Creech, and she was smart enough to know the trade she was making. Besides, I doubted she would end up penniless at the end of this. Whatever poverty was knocking at her door was likely to still leave her wealthier than most in the City.

Unaware of the tiny wheels of judgement turning in my mind, Mrs Creech continued.

"I found him here when I got back, but no sign of whoever killed him." She paused and looked me straight in the eye. "Still, whoever they were, they did me a favour. I don't care about the reasons, so long as this is the end of it."

"Why didn't you call the police or your security team?"

She paused before answering, tilting her head to one side as if she was listening for something. There was a further moment of silence, then she seemed to come to a decision.

"I'm afraid I did, Mr Judas. They should be here any minute."

Her expression didn't change, although there may have been the tiniest hint of regret in her voice. I would have kicked myself for having let my guard down so easily, but by this point, it would be wasted effort. I'd convinced myself that she was about to spill her guts about whatever had been going down between her and her recently deceased husband.

I should have known better. Back in the club, she had moulded herself time and time again into whatever it was people wanted. What I'd wanted was answers, and that's what she'd promised, just long enough to keep me hanging around. I didn't doubt that I was going to be right in the frame for Mr Creech's murder, and being locked up for the next twenty-five years was going to put a major dent in my investigation.

Maintaining my cool is a nice luxury, but one I didn't have the time for, nor was there anyone I was particularly keen on impressing. Stopping only to give Mrs Creech a final nod of acknowledgement, I pushed myself up from the wingback and made for the exit. Whoever she had been listening out for hadn't turned up yet, so there was still a chance I could get out of the mansion's grounds and on my way back to the rougher side of the City before the police arrived. My problems wouldn't exactly end there, but at least it would buy me some time.

That was the plan in my head at least, a plan that went immediately to shit as soon as I pushed myself out of the chair. Rather than making my way briskly across the room, I just toppled slowly forward and ended up with my face pressed into the expensive carpet. My legs had turned to jelly, infused with a warm, calming sensation running through my veins.

"Sorry, Mr Judas, but I can't have my husband's murderer fleeing the scene," Mrs Creech said, placing her own, untouched, glass of whisky back on the small table between the chairs. "Besides, if I'm to be truly free of this life, I need to make sure she gets what she wants."

"Well, that's just fantastic", I thought to myself, as the

warm sensation continued its inexorable rise through my chest and into the back of my eye sockets, willing them to close and accept the comfort of unconsciousness.

The last thing I heard, before whatever drug the drink had been laced with did its trick, was the sound of approaching sirens. Then everything went black.

CHAPTER 23

When I came round, it was to a thumping headache, an unpleasantly bright light, and a sense that I wasn't in Kansas anymore, not that I'm entirely sure what, or where, Kansas is.

"Welcome back to the land of the living, Mr Judas."

Although my eyes were still adjusting to the light, with everything blurry as if my eyeballs had been coated in Vaseline, I was pretty sure that when my vision did return to normal I would be welcomed by the crapulous sight of Sergeant Javan Markos. The mix of boredom and spite in the speaker's voice was unmistakable.

If Markos was there, then you could safely bet his sycophant sidekick Llewelyn would be somewhere nearby. I had run into the pair of them more than once during my colourful career, and we had got on like a house on fire, complete with all the associated property damage, flames, screaming, and running. We have an understanding, they think I'm a trouble-making busybody, and I think they're a pair of incompetent corrupt pricks.

They represented the worst side of the City's small police force. Under the careful tutorship of Chief Harland, law enforcement has become less efficient, but considerably more profitable than it used to be. Not every officer took bribes, looked the other way, or was nestled deep in the pockets of the local politicians or gang-lords, but those who played things straight tended to either see out their relatively short careers as beat cops or retire due to sudden health issues. On the other hand, those who seized all the unique opportunities the job offered rose through the ranks and became deeply unpleasant examples of humanity, like Markos.

I blinked a couple more times, and the last of the blurriness cleared, revealing Markos' unpleasant, pockmarked face leering down at me. As sensation slowly returned to the rest of my body, I could feel the cold steel of handcuffs around my wrists, chained to the table in front of me. It wasn't a reassuring start. I had no memory of anything after Mrs Creech had drugged me, and I was intrigued to know how she had managed to square that one. "Well officers, this dangerous madman scooped out my husband's brains, so I offered him a drink, added some sleeping pills I just happened to have on my person, and hey, presto!"

The problem was cops like Markos and Llewelyn wouldn't be bothered by such little inconsistencies. They favoured simple open-and-shut cases, preferably stuffed full of cash, and I suspected that Mrs Creech was still rich enough to buy, or at least hire, their loyalty several times over.

Now I was fully awake, Markos moved back to the other side of the table and lowered himself into his seat with a grunt. He was wearing his trademark white suit, which I knew he thought made him look suave, setting him aside from the rank-and-file detectives in the force. I thought pale material was a bad choice for a man who could break a sweat sitting completely still in a cold room.

"Happy to have you back with us, Judas," he said, grinning unpleasantly. "I was worried you were enjoying your sleep a little too much. I gotta be honest; I've been looking forward to seeing you sat on that side of the table for a long time. It would have been a real shame for you to snooze through your indictment."

"Glad I could make it," I managed, although my mouth still felt like I'd just come out of a particularly bad trip to the dentists.

"You've messed up for sure this time, Judas," came a second weasel voice from just behind me, which at least confirmed where Llewelyn was. I'd never see him apart from Markos, following him around like a whipped dog. While Markos was professionally unpleasant and crooked as a seven-dollar bill, Llewelyn was a toadying wannabee. There might be a decent detective submerged somewhere under all the slime, but I'd never seen any sign of it. "I've got you in the precinct sweepstake, so putting you away will be a double win."

He circled around me, his suit as shiny and cheap as the man himself. Whatever he was spending his backhanders on, it wasn't clothes... or deodorant. He stopped and leaned back against the wall, fixing me with a hard-eyed stare that I suspected he'd practised for hours in his bathroom mirror. I was tempted to give a worried-looking shiver, just to make him feel better about all that wasted time and effort, but I hadn't got the energy.

I think he was about to speak again, but Markos stepped in, shutting his partner down before he could say anything. It was clear where the power in the room sat, and none of it was with Llewelyn, for all his posturing.

"You pulled on the tail of a tiger this time, Judas," Markos told me, unable to contain the pleasure in his voice. "The Chief asked to be informed personally when you came round. I don't know much about that fella you offed, but she is seriously pissed, so I'm guessing he was quite a guy."

"So, what now?" I asked. "If the Chief wants to speak with me then I guess I can tell you two to go fuck yourselves."

"Why, you smart-mouthed...." Llewelyn began, winding back his scrawny arm for what promised to be one of the more pathetic blows to the face I had suffered over the last few days, but Markos grabbed his wrist well before it reached me.

"Leave him be," he grunted. "By the time the Chief's done with him, he'll be plenty sorry enough. Getting thumped will be a blessing, compared to what's coming his way."

Despite my outward bravado, none of what Markos was saying was filling me with optimism. Harland was an ice-cold bitch, had a reputation for meting out brutal punishments to anyone who got in her way, and was ambitious enough to bend or break pretty much any rule if it would benefit her or her current paymaster.

Over time, she had built up a cadre of detectives in her inner circle who shared her principles. None of them had quite the same level of drive or ambition, and most lacked much in the way of ability, but they all offered what she valued the most, which was unflinching loyalty.

"See you later," Markos said, with a snigger and a two-fingered wave as he left. Llewelyn trailed a couple of steps behind.

It tells you something about an 'interview room' when you're chained to the desk and they feel the need to install a big drain in the corner. I was left alone for a while, presumably to stew a bit, look at the drain and dwell on what was coming my way. The aim was to crank up my anxiety levels, making sure I was ready to curl up and sob out my confession when Harland turned up. Unfortunately for Harland, I had been through at least half a dozen far worse experiences in the last forty-eight hours, so what it mainly did was give me a chance to shut my eyes and try and get my thoughts in order. Although it was hazy, I was sure I could remember Mrs Creech saying something about 'making sure she gets what she wants' just before I'd passed out, and wondered if it was Harland she'd been referring to. With that comforting thought in mind, I settled in to wait.

***

I'd only had the pleasure of seeing Harland in the flesh a couple of times, and on one of those occasions, I had seen more of her than I wanted. When she finally stalked into the room, she gave the impression of someone in a hurry, dealing with something that would normally be way beneath her.

She was looking more like a raptor than ever, hair shaved

short on either side of her head, the remainder of her blonde hair tied back in a short ponytail. It highlighted the angular intensity of her face, strong cheekbones and dark eyes. Her movements were similarly efficient, pared to the bone, nothing wasted. So, when she grabbed me by the hair and bounced my head off the table, I was guessing she had a really good reason.

"You've really fucked up this time, Judas." It was more of a question than a statement, so I kept quiet. Besides, I was too busy swallowing a mouthful of blood to say anything.

"It caused enough fuss at City Hall when Creech was found dead," she continued, wiping her hands disdainfully, presumably making sure there were no residual splatters of my blood staining them. "But we followed your trail backwards and found a whole pile of other bodies. Seems like you've been busy."

"Sorry to disappoint you, but it wasn't me. I was just in the wrong place at the wrong time... twice." My words were slightly muffled by my split lip, which was already beginning to swell, but I think she got the gist of it well enough.

"Not good enough," Harland spat back. She was looking seriously pissed, a vein on one side of her head throbbing angrily. "You messed with the wrong people, in a very big way. There are repercussions..."

It all started to make a bit more sense, and I could see why Harland had decided to deal with me herself. It wasn't very smart, but I decided to push back a bit, and see where it took me.

"I'm guessing you and your boys haven't been justifying your protection money the last couple of days, have you?" I took a small amount of pleasure in the momentary flash of anger in her eyes. My barb had hit home, confirming what I already heavily suspected to be the case. Harland had been in the pocket, or at least the pay, of the Dandy and his associates. The fact that he'd ended up dead wasn't going to reflect well on her, or the value of the protection that she and her circle of crooked coppers were supposed to be providing.

She didn't give a shit if I was guilty or not, but she was desperate to show that she was doing something, otherwise an uncomfortable amount of heat was going to be pointed in her direction. That's why she was down here, talking to me in person. Somewhere in the higher echelons of City Hall, some serious damage limitation was going on, which meant that whatever tiny chance of a fair hearing I might have previously enjoyed had just dwindled to nothing. I was going to get the full weight of the law come down on me, leaving nothing behind, besides a vaguely human-shaped stain on the ground.

"Shut your mouth," she hissed, flexing her fingers and giving me a look of pure hatred. I could tell she was seriously considering bouncing my head off the table again, just for the sheer hell of it. But she had more willpower than I gave her credit for, and managed to limit herself to just punching me in the face... hard.

I could see why the drain in the corner had been installed. We had only been chatting for two minutes and I reckon I could have spat out about a pint of blood. A prolonged conversation with her was likely to be terminal.

"You're not smart enough to have got into this on your own, Judas," she said. I was inclined to agree, although I didn't give her the pleasure. "So, I'll give you one last chance to tell me who you're working for. I'll settle for a name, which I suggest you give me while you're still capable of speech."

I had to admire her cavalier attitude to police procedure. There wasn't even a pretence that anything was going to be done by the book. She was on her own, the interview wasn't being taped, and if the video camera in the corner of the room was recording anything, it was only so she could sell it later.

"Do I get a phone call?" I asked, "or a lawyer?" I paused to wipe my mouth on the part of my sleeve I could still reach with my hands chained. "If not, a doctor would be good."

"Your choice, Judas," Harland said, with a faux-sincere

sigh. "Although you'll wish you took the chance to deal with me." She looked down at her watch. "But I'm out of time, which means you are too."

For a moment I thought she was bluffing, but she got straight to her feet, pausing only to give me one final cuff around the back of the head. She didn't ask me anything, so I guess that last one was just for fun.

She left the room just as abruptly as she had entered, leaving the door open. A moment later Markos and Llewelyn rolled back in. Markos was grinning like a kid on Christmas morning, which meant something pretty crappy was about to happen to me.

Llewelyn unlocked the chain from the table, although my hands remained cuffed together, and pulled me up off the chair, one hand gripping a handful of my jacket. With a less than gentle push he propelled me towards the door.

The two of them frogmarched me down the corridor, drawing a few interested stares from passing colleagues.

"What you got there, Markos?" one of the uniformed officers asked with a grin.

"I'm his new partner," I informed him. "He's decided to dump Llewelyn for someone with a bit more charisma."

I spent the next few dozen steps doubled over, after a particularly solid elbow to the guts, which I suppose served me right for being a smart-arse when I didn't need to be. By the time I was able to stand up straight again we'd reached the rear entrance to the station. It led straight to a fenced compound containing a handful of cars, some bins, and one big shadowy, sinister-looking son of a bitch.

Although he was only a silhouette, I had seen that shape enough times in the last couple of days to recognise him straight away. It also explained why my erstwhile companions were so excited. They probably hadn't met a real-life monster before.

"Cain," I muttered to myself, not best pleased with how my day was working out.

I could feel the nervous excitement drifting off Markos and Llewelyn. They weren't exactly squeaky clean, but compared to Cain they were a couple of Boy Scouts.

Markos kicked me in the back of my legs, and Llewelyn gave the small of my back a final hard push, dropping me to my knees.

Cain didn't even look in their direction, all his attention focused on me.

"Piss off. This is a private matter," he told them, without looking up.

If they were disappointed not to get to watch, they were sufficiently cowed not to show it. The door to the station clicked shut behind them with a worrying finality.

That just left the two of us, for a less than happy reunion. It didn't take long to get down to business.

"You killed my employer," Cain told me, as he cracked his knuckles, making a sound like a steamroller driving over a sack of walnuts. "Normally I wouldn't take it so personally, but I've worked for the Dandy for a long time, so the fact that he's dead reflects rather badly on me."

"Not that you'll believe me," I replied. "But I didn't lay a hand on the Dandy, or Creech. I want to find out who did for them as much as you do."

"You're right, I don't believe you, and I don't care about your reasons," Cain said, with a nasty grin. "Even if I did, it wouldn't make any difference. You've been a boil on my arse for too long, Judas, so whatever else happens, you'll be ending the day dead." His grin widened. "Doesn't mean it has to be quick, though."

I had been working away at the cuffs while he had been

talking, trying to find a weak spot that I could exploit. There wasn't one, there never is, despite what movies might lead you to believe. Nor will a bent paper clip, hair grip, or whatever, crack them open. What will work is a key, which I didn't have.

"How about we settle this man to man, or whatever it is you are?" I said, with rather more bravado than I was genuinely feeling.

Cain pretended to give my offer some thought. "No need," he eventually replied. "Think I'll just skin you here and now. Leave what's left for the police to find, next time they poke their nervous little heads out those doors. I might keep just a little bit as a memento though, seeing as how we're old friends."

Reaching inside his jacket, he pulled out a short, curved knife, with a rounded tip and a dangerously sharp edge. It wouldn't have looked out of place on a butcher's block, so I guess he wasn't lying about the whole skinning thing.

Just then, the rear door to the station opened and two uniformed officers strolled out, one already with a cigarette in his mouth, ready to light. Good luck isn't exactly my constant companion, but on this occasion I was happy to grab whatever opportunity fate decided to throw my way, no matter how slender.

The closest of the two clocked us almost straight away and was bright enough to work out that the big, sinister-looking guy holding a butcher's knife was probably not a paid-up member of the police force. She was pretty quick too, her hand dropping to her sidearm immediately. Unfortunately for her, pretty quick doesn't come anywhere near cutting it when you're dealing with Cain. He was on her before her gun was even halfway out its holster, a splash of crimson spraying the shocked face of her partner, cigarette still dangling from his lips. In a flash, he was down too, Cain's arm moving in a blur.

They were probably two decent cops, they certainly hadn't been counting on meeting Cain, which meant that they weren't part of Harland's dirty little cabal. I should have tried to help them, but the truth is that I was running for the barrier the second I saw them. Even with my arms free, I knew I was no match for Cain. Cuffed, I would just be on more piece of collateral damage.

Sometimes, doing the right thing doesn't mean quite what you might imagine. Stopping to help wouldn't have changed anything, other than adding me to the body count. By running, I had reduced the number of deaths by one and left myself a chance to get some sort of payback, so running was the 'right' thing to do. At least that's what I told myself. I was pretty sure my conscience would be taking the matter up with me later.

Vaulting the barrier was going to be tricky with my hands chained together, so I dropped and rolled under it instead, picking myself up and continuing my mad dash without stopping. I reckoned the two unfortunates who had interrupted us had brought me somewhere between a ten and fifteen-second head-start, which was pretty much fuck all when someone like Cain is on your trail. Lucky for me, I didn't have to go too far.

The old construction site I had scoped out earlier was only a five-minute walk from the station, or a two-minute sprint. Even over that short distance, I wasn't sure I would be able to stay ahead of Cain, but the memory of his flashing blade did a good job of spurring me on.

I hadn't planned on heading there under quite these circumstances, I'd intended to lure Cain across town when I'd had the chance to have a rest and recharge, but I was going to have to settle for facing him after being drugged, interrogated, and repeatedly punched in the face by an angry police chief.

As I turned into the next side street, I caught a glimpse of my destination. It was ugly, derelict, and still one of the most wonderful sights I had ever seen.

"This is getting to be something of a habit," Cain yelled at my back gleefully. "You running, me chasing. It's all a bit boring.

Sooner or later, you'll get tired, slip, whatever… and I'll get to play. Gloves are off now, Mr Judas."

I covered the last few metres in a half stagger, nearly losing my footing on some loose rubble, ending up right in the centre of the building site I had picked out after my visit with Sebastian.

It had taken a while to find just the right spot, and this had been as close as I could get to perfect. Some hopeful conglomerate had chosen this patch of urban wasteland to build a new hotel. They had borrowed a huge amount from some unsavoury business partners, who didn't give two shits if the hotel ever got built but were extremely keen on very complex repayment structures. To my relief, everything was exactly how I'd left it, and I quickly pocketed the small, wrapped package I had left taped to one of the steel struts.

The developer only got as far as erecting the steel skeleton before they ran out of cash, enthusiasm, and breath, in that exact order. Their downfall had been my good fortune, giving me just what I needed, exactly when I needed it. The fact that it was near to the Police Station was a bonus I hadn't foreseen at the time.

To be fair, Cain had a point. I had spent more than my fair share of time in the last couple of days running away from a variety of Daemons, monsters and psychopaths, but this time was different.

"I wasn't running, Cain," I shouted at the approaching figure. "I just wanted to make sure you and I ended up somewhere with plenty of space."

"Why's that then, Judas?" he asked, a high-pitched giggle escaping before he could stop it, tacked on to the end of the question.

"I needed enough room to do this!"

Hoping desperately that my calculations had been at least

vaguely correct, I pulled down hard on the length of chain hanging to my left. There was a moment when nothing happened, and I thought that the previous evening's hard work had been wasted... then there was a rumble and the heavens opened.

Sometimes people talk about it raining buckets, or cats and dogs, but very rarely do they speak about it raining girders. As the first of the lengths of metal slammed into the ground about ten metres away, I realised why. Even though I was expecting it, the whole thing was still very loud, extremely disorienting, and really fucking dangerous.

Even Cain, who as far as I know isn't afraid of anything, looked temporarily confused. Despite that, and his bulk, he still managed to side-step the next falling beam like a ballerina, the pillar of metal that should have impaled him missing him by a matter of inches.

"Nice trick, Judas," he called across, taking a quick step to neatly avoid another of the beams clattering off just to one side.

I was already moving, rushing towards him almost faster than the eye could see. I was Magicked up to the eyeballs and knew that this little burst of speed was going to put me on my back for at least a week somewhere down the line, but it was a price I was more than willing to pay.

It would have been nice if one of my carefully prepared steel columns had speared Cain, but I hadn't ever really expected it to. The guy was too damn fast to get caught out. What it did provide was a big, noisy distraction, which I was praying would be enough for me to get in close enough to carry out the next part of my plan.

Even with everything going on around him, the big, crazy bastard was still moving like a flyweight, dancing between the falling beams like they weren't even there. Even amped up on Magick, I wasn't moving that much faster than Cain, and by the time I reached him, he had turned to face me and was lowering himself into a balanced, fighting stance.

I didn't have time for anything fancy, and my wrists were still shackled, so I settled for slamming my shoulder into the nearest column of metal, toppling it straight at Cain's grinning face. It should have squashed him flat, but somehow he managed to catch it, stopping its progress. He gave a grunt of effort and heaved it back in my direction, but fortunately for me, I had already committed to the next part of my plan and had moved far enough around him for it to pass me by. I still felt the breeze as it whipped past my face, before clattering into further falling columns.

"What's your game, Judas?" Cain shouted. He didn't sound worried, just… interested. It's times like these I wish I was better at snappy answers, but I've never been any good at that type of thing, so I settled for throwing the small, wrapped package I had just recovered, straight at his smug face.

Even then, with him distracted and only a few metres away, I nearly missed, but my luck held and while I missed his face, the package caught the edge of his shoulder, where its contents shattered with a subdued tinkle of breaking glass.

As unnaturally fast as Cain might be, all his exertions meant he was breathing more heavily than normal, and he caught a good slug of my carefully prepared concoction on his next inhalation.

The mix I had been working on was strong enough to sedate an elephant, so I was hoping it would knock Cain straight off his feet. But he was tough as old leather, so, rather than buckling his legs it just slowed him down.

The other side-effect was that he was now seriously pissed at me, the amused grin giving way to an angry snarl. He threw a heavy fist in my direction, slowed by the mix of sedatives, although still far faster than any regular human. He was just far enough away for me to avoid the worst of it, receiving a glancing blow rather than the full force of his attack. It was enough to knock me back, one of the teetering girders missing me by inches.

Cain wasn't so lucky. The fact that he was concentrating on hitting me had taken his attention off the rest of the giant, chaotic game of Jenga going on around us. His snarl turned into a look of puzzlement as one of the heavy beams clipped his shoulder with a stomach-churning crack. Even then, he kept going, but no matter how tough you are, having half the bones in your body broken all at once is going to slow you down, and it was only moments before a second girder caught him.

He sank to his knees with a sigh, still sounding more regretful than pained, presumably upset that he wasn't going to get to pull my spine out as he'd planned. Looking me square in the face, he lifted both huge hands, grinned, and gave me the finger.

Whatever else I thought about him, I had to admit he had balls and a certain horrible style, but that was about as far as my sympathy went.

"This is for Trent, you son of a bitch," I said, as the last of the beams toppled inevitably towards his kneeling body.

There was a spark in his eyes, a reaction. But not the one I was expecting. I had thought he would show one final moment of defiance or scorn, but all I could see was confusion. Whatever momentary sense of victory I had enjoyed vanished in an instant. I had been absolutely sure that Cain had been the one to kill my friend... but I had been certain about the Dandy being behind things too, and that rug had already been pulled from under my feet.

Suddenly I had questions, ones that only Cain could answer. I reached out in one final, and completely futile gesture, as the hard edge of the falling girder crushed his skull like an eggshell.

Everything I had been through over the last few days caught up with me at that moment, and I lost my breakfast, lunch, and whatever else was still sloshing around in my system. The world around me blurred, the pain I had been holding back hitting me in one tsunami of bruised flesh and exhausted nerves. I managed to stagger a few unsteady paces away from Cain's ruptured body, then sank to my knees.

It didn't stop me from passing out, but at least I was a bit closer to the ground, so when my head bounced off the pavement it wasn't all that painful. Not exactly the same as sinking into a pile of well-stuffed pillows, but when you're as tired as I was feeling, even the harsh kiss of concrete can feel strangely comforting.

When I came to, it was well into the night, as you could tell by the change in the sounds bouncing around the streets. The hum of cars had faded away, replaced with the heavy silence that came stalking alongside the dark in some of the worst parts of the City.

My head was pounding, although this was balanced out by the pain running down my right-hand side. Whatever limited reserve of adrenaline that had been keeping me going over the last couple of days was well and truly spent, and every stored-up ache, pain, tear and sprain was making itself known with a vengeance.

CHAPTER 24

Fortunately for me, the taxis that run the streets at night are notoriously open-minded when it comes to their patrons. While I didn't have any actual cash on me to pay for a ride home, I did promise the driver that I would add a healthy tip to pay for the deep clean the upholstery was going to need after I'd leaked all over it. The fact I was still cuffed didn't even register as an issue. You've got to love the place.

The last few steps up to my brand-new door were the hardest part of the journey. I seriously considered setting up base camp between stairs five and six and settling in till dawn, but I dug deep and pressed on to the landing.

The new door was doing an excellent job of keeping the office safe from the rest of the world, but unfortunately, that included keeping me outside, mainly as all my belongings, including my keys, had been taken from me at the station. I hadn't got the energy left for a full-on knock, but I managed a creditable couple of taps.

"Who's there?"

"It's me, Samson, you half-arsed excuse for a fur-ball. Now 'Open Sesame' and let me in."

I knew that the note I had left him earlier hadn't been all that reassuring and that Samson had locked the place up tight on my say so, but even through the thick wood of the door, he sounded nervous as hell.

"Tell you what," he replied, still sounding uncharacteristically shaken. "Tell me something that only you would know, and I'll let you in."

"You told me my blood tastes like shit… oh… and you're an annoying dick."

There was a creak as the door opened a fraction, and one yellow eye glared at me through the gap.

"No need to be mean, Judas," he said reproachfully, before backing away, leaving me to let myself in.

When I stumbled through the door of the office, Samson was doing some very serious pacing. His fur was standing on end, and at the end of each little circuit of the room, he would pause with his back arched. I'm guessing it was the equivalent of a nervous tick, the worried scratch of a head, the unsettled twisting of fingers. It's just that cats tend to be more expressive. If they're pissed off, then their whole body looks angry; when they're scared, every single part of them emanates fear; and when they're nervous, you can see it from space.

"Thank goodness you're back, Pat."

His opening words made it clear there was something important going on. There's no way Samson would normally admit he was glad to see me.

"What the hell's happened to you now?" he added, looking me up and down. "Someone's made a proper mess of your face," he turned his attention to the cuffs still locking my wrists together.

"They look new."

"It's been a busy few hours," I admitted. "Got framed for the murder of Creech, then got my face pummelled by Chief Harland, then topped it all off by killing Cain."

"Shit the bed!" Samson gave a whistle, which still sounds strange coming from a cat. "Don't get me wrong, I won't be crying over Cain, but how the hell did you kill him, I thought the guy was pretty much immortal. Plus, he's already kicked your ass about a dozen times."

"I cheated," I admitted, although without any real shame. "Dropped a tonne of metal straight on his head. To be fair, I was still cuffed, so it's not like he was spoiling for a fair fight."

I needn't have bothered trying to justify myself. Cats aren't fussed about sportsmanship or morals. They care about results, and when you're talking about Cain, him being dead was a good result for absolutely everyone else in the world.

"How about Harland?" Samson added. "She's going to come looking for you. We've got enough trouble without the law coming knocking."

"Don't know, and for the minute, don't care," I replied. "She handed me straight to Cain, so I'm guessing whatever was going on was off the books. For the minute she probably thinks I'm dead, and I'm happy to let her keep believing that for as long as possible."

"Glad we've got all that straight," Samson said. "As long as we're not going to get raided in the next couple of hours. There's some important stuff we need to catch up on."

"First off, I need to get rid of these," I nodded down at the cuffs still chaining my wrists together. "Oh... and could you do me a favour and pop down to pay for the taxi... he's expecting a big tip, too."

Fifteen minutes with an angle grinder was enough to finally release the cuffs, and also gave me a chance to explain to Samson what had been going on, including the look on Cain's face when I had accused him of Trent's death.

"He was an untrustworthy son of a bitch, but he looked genuinely confused. I don't think he did for Trent, and he definitely didn't kill the Dandy. Someone else has been cleaning house."

Samson didn't immediately say anything, but after a minute nodded in the direction of the computer.

"You're not wrong," he said. "I had another look at the

video from the Dandy, while you were out. I think I know who killed them all... and I don't think you're going to like it."

I didn't say anything, presuming he was getting to whatever his point was.

"I must have sat through the whole thing four or five times," he continued, "and it was pretty bloody boring. I thought the Dandy would do more with his time than sit at his desk drinking tea and watching video clips."

So far, so underwhelming. I had worked all that out for myself.

"It was the end of the clip." He turned his back to me, starting his pacing again. "Right at the end, when it all started to go completely to shit. I almost missed it, but something caught my eye."

"I've watched that section a dozen times," I told him, "and there's nothing in the room, just a couple of heavies getting torn to bits, a brief moment when the Dandy looks like he's about to crap himself, then fade to black."

"It wasn't something in the room," Samson replied, turning back to face me, "it was something in the mirror. I didn't see it before, too busy looking at the Dandy."

"Well?"

"Better you see it for yourself." Samson padded his way back to the computer, sat and waited for me to join him.

The last moments of the Dandy's life were there on the screen, forever frozen in time. He was caught with his hand partway to his desk drawer, eyes fixed on something just out of sight... or so I had assumed. Maybe cat's eyes were just better for this type of thing. The scene in the room was pretty dark, but I guess that wasn't too big a deal for Samson.

I stared at the mirror behind the desk, trying to spot whatever it was that Samson had seen. There was definitely something there, something I had perhaps seen but failed to recognise when I had reviewed the recording. If I squinted, it could even be the shape of a person, but I couldn't make out enough to get any more from it.

"Okay, there's something there… but I can't see what it is. I suppose you're going to tell me?"

"Better than that," Samson replied, a touch of his natural feline smugness reasserting itself. "I'm going to show you, although, like I said, I don't think you are going to like it."

He padded across to the printer, which was still on the floor, one of the few things that had survived the raid on the office largely unscathed. Probably because it was nearly as old as I was, weighed a ton, and was made of a mysterious yellowing plastic that appeared impervious to pretty much anything.

"It took a while," Samson added, "and a little more help from Gaby." He hurried on with his explanation, leaving no opening for me to protest. "Face facts, Pat, she's better at this sort of thing than either of us. She was able to brighten up the image enough for even your pathetic human eyes."

"Dammit, Samson," I growled, "I left her out of this deliberately. I wouldn't have gone to that prick Sebastian otherwise."

Samson gave a particularly expressive shrug, managing to convey the fact that he didn't care, and that actually I was the prick for not going to Gaby in the first place. It was hard to argue with that kind of aggressive body language.

"Fine, what did you two dig up that's so important?"

Samson tilted his head in the direction of the most recent print laying alongside the printer. It contained a single image, a magnification of the clip from the camera footage centred on the mirror. Whatever it was that Gaby had done looked like it had worked. What had been too dark and indistinct to make out was now clear enough to recognise. Not perfect, but sufficient to take the air out my lungs and leave my head spinning.

The face in the mirror was one that I recognised, although not the expression of violent intent. The mouth that had worked a gentle enchantment was twisted in a snarl of rage, eyes that had pleaded for help, now narrow and hard.

"Eve..."

"Yup," Samson said, not unkindly. "Bit of a shitter really. And there I was thinking she was such a nice girl. Turns out she has a bit of a dark side."

CHAPTER 25

Describing tearing through a platoon of highly trained body-guards and then scooping out the insides of the Dandy's head as 'a bit of a dark side' seemed like an understatement, but I could see the point Samson was making.

"So, now what are we going to do?" Samson asked. "For a start, she phoned for you earlier. Said she wanted to speak to you. Judging from all of this, I doubt it was for a purely social visit."

He looked back down at the photo and shuddered. "I quite like all my internal organs where they are, and I'm developing trust issues as far as Eve is concerned."

What I wanted to do next was rest, take about a year off to really work all the kinks out of my system. Merle had taught me, at great length, how to manage the effects of Magickal expenditure, including the kind of exhaustion and pain I was now experiencing, although I had never been very good at that particular lesson. It required the practitioner to enter into a kind of semi-trance state, applying the age-old rule of mind over matter in a very literal sense. Unfortunately for me, being in pain was too much of a distraction to do any sort of complicated mental trickery, so in the past, I had generally settled for getting seriously drunk and trying not to get sober until I was fixed.

I didn't have that luxury. When I had first spoken to Barbara, she had told me that Eve was due to be sent down in the Elevator in less than three days. My perception of time had been pretty messed up by a lack of sleep and at least one period of involuntary unconsciousness, but by my calculations, more than two of those days had already passed, which meant I was rapidly running out of time. Tempting as it might be, doing it drunk wasn't going to work.

I couldn't escape the feeling that whatever was going to go down would happen at the Elevator. Creech was dead, so the swap, or whatever it was, with Eve was presumably off, but I knew that wouldn't be the end of it. My instinct that Eve was the cause of all the chaos over the last couple of days had been right, in a way. It's just I had assumed she was the victim, not the perpetrator.

"I need to go to the Elevator," I told Samson. "Tonight."

"Rather you than me," Samson replied with a shrug. "That place gives me the creeps at the best of times. Add whatever that girl is to the mix and I'm staying well clear... no offence."

"Wish me luck, then," I said.

"You'll need more than luck, Pat..." Samson shouted after me as I made my way out. I guess he was trying to be helpful, but his pep-talk definitely needed work.

I had only made it halfway to the Elevator when the combination of painkillers and adrenaline that had been keeping me moving gave a stutter and I was hit by a wave of pain and nausea.

Closing my eyes, I summoned my chi, centred my being, got in touch with my spirit animal, cleansed my aura, and became one with my breath. All of which achieved a sum total of fuck all, as I hadn't got a clue how to do any of those things.

I'm not even sure I have an aura. If I did, I suspect that cleansing it would require a specialist team with the psychic equivalent of bleach and at least a week of hard scrubbing.

Muttering under my breath that Magick was a crock of shit and cursing the day I ever discovered it, I knocked back the two remaining happy pills that had kept me moving for the last twenty-four hours, and hoped for the best.

Aside from whatever nasty side effects might be waiting for me in the wings, I had to admit they were pretty good. Within a few minutes, I was able to walk in a vaguely straight line without bursting into tears, which seemed like a good start.

I could see the spire of the Elevator off in the distance, so I set my sights on the top of the glass tower and set off at a run. It hurt more than I'm able to explain, but the painkillers were only going to work for the next hour or so, so whatever I was going to do had to be done before then.

It might have been the effect of the tablets, putting a layer of cotton wool between me and the rest of the world, but as I ran through the increasingly populated streets, I had never felt more disconnected from the City. I saw a couple walking arm in arm, leaving a late-night diner. They looked happy, totally ignorant of the darkness just beneath the surface all around them. They didn't look like they had ever faced Daemons or walked in on hollowed-out crime lords. I envied them, managing to find a centre of normality even in a place like this, able to rationalise or ignore anything that threatened the perception of the City they had managed to create for themselves.

Fortunately, I managed to reach the vast tower that housed the Elevator before I sank any deeper into self-pity. I checked my watch. It was less than fifteen minutes to midnight.

The foyer of the building was brightly lit as always, and I could see Barbara stationed behind the reception desk. For a moment, my feverish mind stumbled down a random rabbit hole, wondering if she ever did anything else. Every single time I had been to the Elevator she had been there, and I work some pretty weird hours. If it had been anyone else, I would have assumed that they would need to rest, or sleep, or... something, but I was beginning to suspect that Barbara did none of those things.

"Welcome back, Pat," she said, without even looking up. The fact that I was about two small steps away from unconsciousness and covered in blood didn't seem to bother her in the least.

"Hi, Barb." I waggled the fingers of my right hand in a pathetic attempt at a wave.

"You look in a bad way," she added, more as a statement of fact than a question, "and you look like you need a drink."

I nodded. Barbara was right, as always. I did need a drink, a really big one. It's just I couldn't have one, because I needed to… I needed to…

I couldn't remember what it was I needed to do, but I was sure it was really, really important.

My last two painkillers had bailed on me, stripping away the limited comfort I had been hiding behind, leaving nothing but pain and confusion. There was too much pressing in on my overloaded brain for me to think of anything other than the need to close my eyes, preferably for good.

I'm not sure how she managed it, but the next moment Barbara was next to me, catching me as my knees buckled. She pressed a small glass vial into my unresisting hand.

"I meant it when I said you need a drink," she said. "But maybe something a bit more sensible than your normal choice. Try this."

She had to guide the vial to my lips, but as soon as she did, I could feel my head clearing. I had no idea what was in it, but just the fumes were blowing the cobwebs from my brain.

As the first drops of the liquid hit my throat I would have screamed if I had the energy, it was like taking a swig of lava, washed down with an acid chaser, all pushed down my throat by a swarm of angry bees using wire brushes.

"What the bloody hell is this?" I croaked when I regained the ability to talk.

"It's a little pick-me-up that I save for special occasions," Barbara said with the slightest twist of her lips. If I didn't know better, I would have sworn that the bottom half of her face was attempting a smile, but without the benefit of ever having successfully managed one previously.

"Has Eve… is she…"

"No. You still expecting to see her, then?" Barbara said. "I checked the book earlier tonight and her name's gone. And I don't mean gone from tonight's schedule, I mean gone completely." She grimaced in annoyance, obviously angry that someone was messing with her orderly existence. "I guessed you might still turn up, though. You've got a stubborn way about you, Pat. Makes you a thorn in my side, but a reliable one."

Whatever it was that Barbara had given me was doing incredible things to my insides. The initial burning sensation was fading and leaving behind a body that felt almost human again. I looked down at my right arm, which a few minutes before had been hanging next to useless by my side, and flexed my fingers. When I looked back up, Barbara was back in her normal spot, behind the reception desk. How she'd covered that distance in such a short time was a mystery I would have to ponder another time.

"I don't like it when people try and mess with the order of things," Barbara said, tapping away at her keyboard once again. "You and I might come from very different places, Judas, but I think that's something we have in common. Whatever you might think of the rules that run the City, they exist for a reason. At the end of your time here there is reward or punishment. The Elevator decides, and no-one should have the power to change that."

"Funny you should say that," I replied. "I think I've finally got to the bottom of what's been going on, and there's a small favour I wanted to ask."

Barbara gave me an unimpressed look, but she didn't immediately shut me down either. Taking her silence as a willingness to at least listen to what I had to say, I headed across to the desk and told her my plan. Or at least, the collection of thoughts that had been bouncing around in my head ever since I had killed Cain.

Plan is probably too strong a word. Even describing what I had in my head as thoughts was pretty optimistic, but it was all I had.

"You realise what you are asking, Judas?" Barbara began. "If you're wrong…"

She paused, her attention taken up by something behind me.

"Ah, right on time."

The voice was immediately recognisable, and yet at the same time totally alien. I looked back across my shoulder, and there, framed in the glass doorway of the atrium, was the unmistakable sight of Eve. Or at least, the young woman who walked into the building had her face, but everything else about her was different. The gentle smile, the nervous expression, the hesitant walk, all of them were gone, replaced instead with the confident swagger of someone used to being in charge.

It was like seeing a familiar landscape from a completely different perspective. From one viewpoint all you can see is a lush valley, tall trees, and gentle hills, but if you move and view it from somewhere new, you can see the fetid swampland that the trees had been hiding.

"Glad you could make it, Judas," she continued, ignoring Barbara completely, focusing all her attention on me, as if we were the only two people in the world. A few days ago, I might have fallen for it, would have revelled in her attention, but now I felt like someone waking from a dream. A dream in which the beautiful promises it offered were darker and more dangerous than any nightmare, made all the more deadly by their apparent innocence.

I had a hundred questions, piled on top of each other, so heavy that the weight of them threatened to break my back.

"You knew I'd be here?"

She smiled indulgently.

"Of course. You're nothing if not predictable, Judas. Tough old Private Eye, trying to make good his mistakes. You're driven more by guilt than you realise."

She turned to Barbara, acknowledging her existence for the first time, as she continued.

"Did you know he still thinks about that girl he let die all those years ago? That it still eats him up. That he did nothing to bring her murderers to justice."

Another piece of the puzzle slotted into place, and I realised why Eve's face was familiar to me. It wasn't the same, but there were obvious similarities now I was looking for them. The wide mouth, the nervous smile, the hint of freckles across her cheeks. I hadn't consciously picked up on it until now, but there were little things about her features and personality traits that made me think of Katya, the girl who had been found dead in the docks after hiring me. The girl I had failed to protect.

"Guilt is a great motivator," Eve said, turning back to me. "You let that poor young girl die and didn't do a thing, but it stuck with you, even after all this time, didn't it? I wonder if you still see her face when you sleep. All I had to do was play the damsel in distress, remind you of her, and you were like putty in my hands."

As she spoke, I could have sworn that her face rippled for a moment, the smiling lips parting to reveal something older beneath the surface, and then it was gone.

"Everyone has their own little set of levers, Judas," she said, turning away from me and strolling towards the bank of elevators, hands in the pockets of her dark cargo pants. "Some like money, some want power, some have dirty little secrets they would go to any lengths to hide… but, to my surprise you turned out to be more complex. Far more so than I would have thought, looking at your sorry excuse for a life. There's very little that you care about, and none of it relates to your wellbeing, so I had to dig a bit deeper. Who would have thought that there were still the remains of a good man buried under all that booze and misery?"

I didn't answer. There was no point, I wouldn't be telling Eve anything she didn't already know. To know about Katya she either had to be amazingly well connected, or something more than human, and of the two options I was leaning towards the second. Besides, there were questions I had for her, and I needed answers, one way or another.

"I saw you in the video from the Dandy's place. You killed him and his men like they were nothing, and I'm guessing you killed Creech, too."

She nodded, almost absent-mindedly, hardly acknowledging that we were talking about cold-blooded murder, but she didn't answer. Then I asked the question that mattered to me the most.

"...and Trent, was he another one of yours?"

I had hoped for some sign of contrition, or at least some sort of reaction when I mentioned Trent. The others maybe had it coming. They had been playing a dangerous game, attempting to corrupt what passed for natural justice in the City. They had paid the ultimate price, and the world was no sadder for their passing, but Trent... Trent had been a good man, an innocent sucked into whatever grand game had been bubbling away beneath the surface.

But Eve's face showed nothing, no remorse, no sorrow, no emotion at all. Instead, she just looked down at her hands, delicate fingers stretched out in front of her, flexing slightly.

"Fragile little things," she mused. I guessed she wasn't talking about her hands, but rather what they had taken. There was a terrible strength in those slim digits. I had seen the results of her handiwork, ripping through the Dandy's security like they were papier mâché dolls.

Whatever glamour she had been exuding whenever I had met her before was still there. I could feel the urge to believe her, protect her – sacrifice myself for her if necessary – welling up uninvited. I had been so certain of her innocence that I had willingly burned every bridge and played every card I had left, determined to do one decent thing.

But everything I had been through over the last few days had put one final layer of scar tissue over feelings that had already been close to dead, and my subconscious was screaming at me, reminding me of the glimpse I had seen of something terrible hiding behind her smile.

"Trent was necessary to commit you to the cause, Judas," she said. "To play your part we needed you to be convincing, and when I killed Trent it gave you a purpose, made you believable."

My fists clenched, fury flooding my veins as I looked at the woman who had taken my friend's life so easily, and who looked back on his death with so little regard, stripping away the cosy candyfloss mist that had been threatening to envelop me.

"And you've done well," she said, sounding disgustingly sincere. "Much better than we ever hoped. Things in the City were tipping too far in the Dandy's favour, and you helped bring back balance."

I was trying to keep my face neutral, but her sham sincerity was more than I could take.

"I'm not your pawn... and there is nothing that could balance out the death of a good man like Trent."

I knew Eve could gut me like a rabbit without breaking a sweat, but I was beyond caring.

"You led me on your pretty little jelly-bean trail all over the City, doing your dirty work. I've lost friends, good people, just so you can gain some advantage, score a few points in whatever game it is you're playing."

Eve nodded, the beatific smile never leaving her pretty mouth. "It's true, now we will have that little bit more control in the City, but isn't it better this way?"

Maybe taking out people like the Dandy would make the City a slightly better place, it would be hard to make it much worse without going around and randomly stabbing people to death with sharpened puppies, but that wasn't the point. The entire city was built on the foundations of free will, a second chance for people who had fucked up their life. True, plenty just used the opportunity to make an even more spectacular mess this time around; but there were also those trying to make something of themselves, make better choices, and eventually earn a ride on the Elevator when their time came.

As far as I could see, the whole system was in danger of being sucked up and spat out as part of whatever great war was being played out in the background. Free will doesn't count for anything if someone has a hand shoved up your ass, working you like a puppet.

My face might not be that pretty, but it is expressive, and what I was thinking was playing out so clearly that it cut through whatever self-righteous glow Eve had going on.

"You really don't get it, do you?" she said, the soft caramel of her voice that had charmed me before, now overly sweet and cloying.

"You were lucky enough to be chosen. Selected to do something good for this forsaken place. It's a City full of broken souls, where the cruel and the strong thrive, clambering over everyone else to get what they want and robbing others of what they deserve. How can you even contemplate defending them?"

It was a fair question, and I didn't have an answer. All I knew was that what Eve was offering wasn't the answer either.

"So, what now?" I asked. For all her talk of me having been

chosen to do something good, the chances of me walking away from this meeting were zero, and we both knew it. She was just taking a moment to justify herself before she did a number on me, the same as she had the others. Oddly, I wasn't as bothered about what would happen to me, as what she might try and do to Barbara. Leaving witnesses didn't seem to be her style.

I checked my watch. It was two minutes to midnight, and I could feel the atmosphere thickening, the hairs on my arms starting to prickle.

"Well, it's been fun, Mr Judas," Eve said, "but I like things tidy. It's nothing personal."

Her face rippled again, giving me another snatched glimpse of whatever was living just beneath the surface, then she was on me, moving faster than I could have imagined possible. One moment I was standing, facing her. The next I was on my back, staring up at the ceiling of the office atrium through watering eyes.

Rather than finish me there and then, Eve let me clamber painfully to my feet. My breathing was ragged, and I could feel something rubbing uncomfortably inside my chest. For all her shiny-faced talk of doing good, I think she was enjoying herself, savouring the moment.

Still, thanks to Merle and a lifetime of training, dedication and bad choices, I still had a trick or two of my own, so when she dashed at me again I was slightly more prepared. Whatever it was that Barbara had given me to drink earlier had juiced me right up, and I could almost feel the Magickal energy spilling out of me, clamouring to be set free.

I slipped into the gaps between seconds, time slowing down around me, and this time I could see Eve coming at me. Even with the rest of the world blurred and heavy around me, she was unnaturally fast. Moving at this speed made it harder for her to keep up the façade of humanity that she had been hiding behind up until now, the pretty, freckled face moving a fraction of a second behind the shadowy, snarling form that was heading for me.

One hand whipped out, snake fast. Long, prehensile fingers topped with bony claws visible beneath the camouflage of slim, delicate digits. Even in my amped-up state, I only just pulled my head back in time to avoid having my face taken off. The tip of one long nail grazed my cheek, opening a long, shallow cut. It was easy to see how the Dandy had ended up like a novelty piñata, those claws could shear through flesh and bone like butter.

It hurt like hell, far worse than it should have, more like the burn of acid than a clean cut. Still, at least I knew what I was facing now. She was a Pride Daemon, one of the rarest of the monstrosities that sometimes walked the City, and also one of the worst. I should have seen it before, the complete, unshakable belief in what she was doing, the willingness to sacrifice others to achieve her goal, and the hungry bestial reality snarling just beneath the attractive exterior.

Pride Daemons secrete a nasty venom that coats their claws and fangs. I had been the unlucky recipient of a minor graze from one of their kind years ago and had only just escaped with my life. I had ended up bed-bound for over a week, vomiting and shivering, weak as a baby kitten, and I had never forgotten the feeling of its poisonous touch.

I reckoned I had a couple of minutes before the cut I'd just suffered put me on my back, and maybe another couple again until I lost consciousness. Trying to make the most of the time I had left, I backed away from Eve, moving within time, pushing myself through the gaps in the still air of the atrium.

The fact that I was wounded wasn't lost on Eve, and there was an eagerness in her movements as she narrowed the distance between us. I was close to the bank of elevators by now, able to feel, even if not see, their presence behind me, leaving me with nowhere else to run.

There wasn't much point in staying ahead of her now, so I let go of the Magick that had been wrapped around me and felt the world snap back to normal. At the same moment, Eve's closed fist slammed into my stomach, knocking me back against the cold metal of the elevator doors.

I should have been grateful that it hadn't been her claws this time, still shimmering half-seen below the outer shell of humanity, but I was too busy feeling sorry for myself. It felt like half my face was on fire, a baby elephant had tap-danced across my ribs, and now my stomach was trying to work its way out of my body via my throat.

So, instead of feeling grateful, I just lay propped against the wall and did my best not to pass out. Everything was blurry, fading from the edges of my vision, the venom doing its job. Eve loomed over me, stopping to brush her sleeve where a couple of droplets of my blood had stained it. I don't think she was that bothered by them, but it gave her the opportunity to gloat a little longer before finishing me. It was then that I spotted the small clasp she wore, white gold, in the shape of a dove, and everything clicked into place.

Before she could say anything there was a deep, heavy clang. The sound of the Church bells in the distance striking midnight. It wasn't a usual sound for this time of night, but the little congregation had come together to mourn Trent. If I'd had a glass I would have raised it. Instead, I held the thought of my old friend close, as my eyesight continued to darken.

I was waiting for Eve to lean in for the final blow, but she was looking past me, her eyes widening in surprise, then alarm, then outright fear.

"No..." she snarled. "How... how could this be? Creech is dead, the deal was broken."

I managed a smile, or at least with the half of my face that was still working.

"You might think you're the smartest thing in the room, but you made a real rookie mistake Daemon," I told her, relieved that things had kind of worked out the way I hoped. "You messed with the wrong person."

"Ha... you think too highly of yourself, Judas. You're a waste of skin," she hissed back.

"Oh, not me, I'm impossible to underestimate," I replied with a dry laugh. My voice was getting weak, the poison working its way deeper into my system and beginning to shut things down. "I was talking about Barbara. Underestimating her was the last mistake you'll ever make."

Eve turned her attention from me to the distant figure of Barbara, still sat behind the reception desk, the heavy ledger open in her hands. I couldn't see from this distance, but if I had been closer then I can guarantee what you'd see was the name 'Eve' written back into the departures column, right next to where it had previously been crossed through. I hadn't been sure if asking Barbara to put the name back would do anything at all, or exactly how far Barbara's influence went, but judging from the ominous glow bleeding out from the open door of the elevator just behind me, it had worked out just fine.

Eve took a step towards the desk, arms outstretched, eyes blazing with fury. I was impressed that she achieved even that. It was more than I had ever seen anyone manage, once the Elevator was calling their name. That was as far as she got, though. Her next step was backwards, unwilling and fighting every inch of her own body, towards the yawning open maw of the Elevator.

As she got closer, the pull of the Elevator began to do odd things to the rest of her. The surface glamour that had shielded her true form from the world stripped away, layer by layer. What was left behind was not at all pretty. If you took a skeleton, covered it in a combination of wasted muscle, mould and sharp things, that's pretty much what an unadorned Pride Daemon looks like.

Eve, or whatever her real name was, was still fighting the inevitable, crouched low, her long nails digging a groove into the smooth marble floor of the atrium as she was dragged backwards. She lifted her head and fixed me with a stare so toxic I could feel it burning the parts of me not already overflowing with poison.

There was a sharp, unnerving crack as one of the long claws broke, enough for Eve to lose her desperate grip, and she spiralled back into the waiting embrace of the open elevator door, as it closed slowly over the sound of her defiant screams. Then there was a gentle ping as the doors met, the red glow that had illuminated the atrium fading away, and the Elevator began its inexorable journey.

"Said you shouldn't have messed with Barbara," I muttered through numb lips.

That's the thing with Pride Daemons... over-confident.

I would have celebrated the way things turned out. But my arms and legs had already completely given up on me, and the pain in the rest of my body had faded to a cool numbness, suggesting that several important organs had just shut down.

It wasn't exactly how I had imagined things ending. But then again, anyone who'd imagine anything even slightly like this had bigger psychiatric problems to deal with, so I didn't feel too bad.

The Church bell was still clanging in the background, so the whole thing with Eve and the Elevator must have taken less than twelve strikes. It seemed pretty fitting somehow, and there was a smile on my face as unconsciousness claimed me.

Whether it was the poison coursing through my system or simply my brain stubbornly pushing back against the looming prospect of my imminent death, rather than sinking into blissful blankness, my unconscious mind was a flickering sea of imagery. I would have preferred oblivion, but you don't always get what you want.

CHAPTER 26

As I've said before, my subconscious mind is often a better detective than I am, and it was making the most of being in charge. I wasn't going to be doing anything else for a while, so, rather than try to fight it, I sat back and let the images play out as my mind spiralled, an endless staircase to wherever.

Instead of concentrating on Eve, the first place my brain chose to take me was my meeting with Mrs Jones. I remembered the careful breadcrumb trail of tiny encouragements that she had threaded through our conversation, just enough to convince me to hand over the leverage I had on Chief Harland. I could still visualise the deep purple of her gown, and at the back of my mind the shape of her brooch, a dove in flight, illuminated by the lamp over her desk.

Then the scene shifted, and I was sat with Mrs Creech, the same brooch glistening in the light of the library as she calmly told me about the brutal murder of her husband, before she tried to feed me to the sharks.

The clasp that Eve had been wearing was almost identical, once again the sign of a dove on the wing. I hadn't paid it too much attention to start with, too busy trying to keep my face from being ripped off, but in the final moments when Eve had been looming over me I realised it was the same symbol, and everything had started to fall into place.

It made sense, in an awful way. Pride Daemons, powerful as they are, don't run things. They're a tool to be used. A hugely dangerous, psychopathic tool, but a tool nonetheless. That meant that Eve wasn't the mastermind behind what had been going on, she was the muscle. Nor did Mrs Creech strike me as being the power player in all of this. She was smart and dangerous enough, but she didn't have the clout or the connections.

Besides, despite all the lies and deceit, I was still sure that there had been a core of truth in what Mrs Creech had told me. Whatever games were being played, more than anything she had wanted to be free of her husband. I suspected that the cost of her freedom had ended up being far steeper and bloodier than she'd imagined.

That left Mrs Jones, and much as I hated to entertain the thought, deep down I knew it made a lot of sense. I had put off seeking her help for a reason, knowing there was always a price to be paid and a game being played in the background. Her club had been at the centre of the City's underworld for a long, long time. A vast web, strands tingling with every conceivable deal and double-cross, and sat right of the centre of it all, her influence had grown.

I'd been struggling to see where I fitted into the whole sorry story. Mrs Jones didn't do anything without a good reason. Every benefit and every risk were balanced and assessed to the most minuscule level.

My mind wandered back to the last time I had been to the Club, the spotlight picking out the petite singer who'd entranced the room for a few wonderful minutes.

It was then the realisation hit. This time around I was the performer, the spotlight focused on me since the first moment Eve had walked into my office and asked for help. Mrs Jones had been planning a war, but if the Dandy had become aware of her plans too early it would have been fatal. When there had been a chance of that spotlight drifting away, she had arranged for Trent's death, bringing all that attention back to me once again.

I thought she had been taking a risk to help me, but handing me the Dandy hadn't cost Mrs Jones a thing. She'd already set her sights on him, a competitor who sat squarely between her and unparalleled influence across most of the City. The fact that Ezekiel had been able to lay his hands on exactly what I needed to find my way to the Dandy's hiding place so quickly should have set off some sort of alarm bell, but I'd been so consumed with my grief for Trent and my hunger for revenge that I'd ignored the warning signs.

Instead, she had put me centre stage, feeding me just enough information to bumble my way towards the version of the truth she wanted me to find. While the Dandy's attention, and that of Cain, had been misdirected, Mrs Jones had been consolidating, increasing her reach. By the time she'd pointed me in the direction of the Dandy's warehouse, she was ready to strike, sending Eve ahead of me to do her dirty work.

I had made just enough noise in all the right places to keep everyone distracted. Worst thing was I'd believed in what I was doing. I had genuinely felt I was doing something good, helping someone who deserved to be helped, someone decent. That belief had made me convincing in the role that Mrs Jones had picked out. Enough to get Barbara to help me, enough even for Cain to mark me as the biggest threat to his boss. It also meant I would have been the first point of call when the police came looking, leaving Mrs Jones safely hidden in the shadows.

I thought back to the time I had stood on the club's balcony, watching the ebb and flow of the crowds below. When I had seen the Dandy and his ever-expanding sphere of influence, the giving and taking of favours, a tiny, grubby eco-system, I was looking for patterns. Mrs Jones had seen opportunities.

Perhaps it was my fault for not thinking big enough. It explained why Mrs. Jones had looked a little disappointed when we left the balcony that night, the lesson she hoped I was learning passing me by. Maybe it had been all the way back then when she had decided, realised that I wasn't going to be a partner in whatever scheme she had in mind. Instead, I would be a tool, something to be used and then disposed of. Whatever passing affection or responsibility she had felt for me could never outweigh her ambition, and I doubt she had lost too much sleep when she decided I had become a liability, rather than an asset.

Even this last showdown with Eve had played into her hands. Either Eve took me down, clearing one more inconvenient obstacle from her path, or I took Eve out, which meant that Mrs Jones was no longer in the debt of a Pride Daemon. I was seriously pissed, but it was hard not to feel some grudging admiration for the sheer scale of ambition and planning.

I had tried my hand at chess a few times when visiting Trent and found out very quickly that I didn't have the mind for it. I was decent enough at taking individual pieces, but terrible at planning more than a couple of moves ahead. On more than one occasion I'd been sure I was about to win, having far more pieces left on the board than Trent did, and then he would pull off one seemingly innocuous move and leave me stuck in checkmate.

Gifted amateur that he might have been, compared to Mrs Jones he was no more than a beginner. Those lazy, flat eyes of hers would have seen every move playing out before the board was even set up.

Behind all the swirling thoughts careering around the inside of my head was the implacable reality of the Elevator. Whatever carnage Eve had managed to wreak upon the world, however smart a game Mrs Jones had played, the Elevator still extracted its toll in the end. It had taken Eve, and eventually, it would come for the rest of us. Now that I had Eve's poison running through my veins, it seemed like I would be next on the list. I would have felt sad, but I guess it had been a long time coming in my case.

One moment it was there, off in the distance at the back of my mind, the narrow spire of the tower rising from the squalor of the City – the next, I was right in front of it, the bank of elevators directly before me. There was a gentle light bleeding out between the closed doors of the central lift and I had the overwhelming desire to reach out.

I wasn't afraid, although I had no sense of what would be awaiting me. My fingers brushed the cold metal. There was a gentle ping and the tiny sliver of light widened as the door began to open.

Whatever else the elevator contained, I had an overwhelming sense that I would find some sort of conclusion, a reason for everything. It might be good, it might be bad, but whatever was waiting would be a change from the daily grind of the City.

The light grew ever brighter until I could see nothing else, and there, right in the centre of it, surrounded by a halo of brightness was... Barbara?

"Judas... wake up, Judas."

I bolted upright with a shuddering gasp, the image of the Elevator disappearing in an instant as the reality of the world came crashing back.

Barbara was kneeling by my side, a syringe in her hand. Judging from the pain in my chest and the fact my shirt was open to the waist, I was guessing she'd just used it on me. The foyer of the building was back to normal, the brightly illuminated Elevator of my feverish mind replaced with the blandly innocent sight of the bank of lifts at the end of the room.

"I thought we'd lost you there for a minute, Judas," Barbara said, getting to her feet and walking back across to the reception desk, "but it seems you aren't quite ready to leave yet."

I wasn't sure I agreed. My recent vision was still fresh and raw in my mind, and the feeling that had coursed through me as I reached out for the light was equally vivid. For that split second, I had been ready, completely willing to find out what the universe had in store for me. But I guess I would be waiting a little longer.

"Thanks, Barb," I replied, with as much sincerity as I

could muster. "Looks like I owe you."

She gave me a withering look as I clambered to my feet and tried to tuck the scraps of material that used to be my shirt back into the waistband of my trousers. Whatever else the last few days had done to me, I was going to need some new clothes.

"You don't owe me anything, Pat," she said, as she began to tap away at her keyboard once again. "Things got out of hand for a while, and we sorted it. Sometimes there are just things that have to be done, and this time it was you that had to do them, that's all."

That seemed like a fairly anti-climactic way to describe everything that had recently gone down, but maybe Barbara dealt with this kind of thing more regularly than I gave her credit for. She certainly didn't seem in the least ruffled by events.

"I've booked you a taxi," she added. "You look like you could do with a rest. Maybe you should take it easy for a few days."

I nodded, although mainly to myself. That sounded like an excellent idea. A quick taxi ride back to the office, incinerate my clothes, maybe have some breakfast, and then sleep... for about a month.

When the cab pulled up outside, I gave Barbara one final wave, but she was busy looking down at her screen, and I'm not sure she even noticed me leave.

CHAPTER 27

A week had passed, and I'd heard nothing more. There was no knock at the door from the police, no late-night call from Ezekiel. It seemed that Mrs Jones had decided to leave me in peace for the moment. She'd got what she wanted from me, and perhaps she had other, more pressing, priorities. After all, there was a whole City to run.

But I knew this window of calm wouldn't last forever. I had seen behind the curtain, knew too much, and sooner or later she would send someone to shut me down for good.

Still, tomorrow was another day, and I would just have to deal with whatever she threw my way when it happened. Mrs Jones might have half of the City's underworld under her control, plus a tight leash on the Chief of Police and a direct line to the corridors of power, thanks to me. But I had a talking cat, a brand-new front door, and half the bottle of bourbon that Ezekiel had gifted me last time I'd visited the Club.

The way I looked at it, we were about even.

The End

Printed in Great Britain
by Amazon

60090790R00121